❋ HALF LIFE

Sarah Gray

Claret
pr@ss

CLARET PRESS

Copyright © 2016 Sarah Gray
The moral right of the author has been asserted.

Cover design by Ginny Wood
Cover and story illustrations © 2016 Alodie Fielding
www.thecrookedstyle.com

ISBN paperback: 978-1-910461-17-4

ISBN ebook: 978-1-910461-22-8

This paperback or the ebook can be ordered from all
bookstores and from Claret Press, as well as eplatforms
such as Amazon and ibooks.

www.claretpress.com

Works by the same author

SURFACE TENSION

For Jonathon

Acknowledgments

Gratitude and love to Katherine Isbester for going beyond the role of editor and making me feel we have good work to do, and that life is worth living despite the circumstances. To my friend Laura Emsden for giving constant support during the writing process and her never-failing belief in the outcome. This is in addition to her insightful feedback and proofreading skills. Enormous thanks also to Alodie Fielding for yet again providing stunning artwork. I couldn't imagine the stories without it. To my family and friends for your enthusiasm and support. Special thanks to: Jonathon Cartwright-Tickle, James Gray, Jane Gray, ML Hindmarch, Nathalie Hounsgaard, Emma Howarth, Ginny Wood and Susan Worley.

Contents

✻

HALF LIFE

From the day Adelaide Anderson was diagnosed,
it took three years, two months, one week and four
days for her to die. She was thirty-six.

*****

Adelaide had told her husband and sister she would haunt them if she had the chance. She had said this sitting in the overcrowded phlebotomy waiting room, immediately after the news that her condition was possibly terminal. The consultant, Dr Wells, had said it would be difficult for Adelaide to think of anything but the worst-case scenario, but she should nonetheless focus on the fact that the outcome wasn't certain. After her declaration to become a ghost, her sister had given a nervous half-laugh and said that she didn't want Adelaide to do anything to scare her. Adelaide had agreed, but said she'd move things around her home just to confuse her. And laughed too. Her husband, Simon, had told her not to be morbid and reminded her that the consultant wasn't sure. It was possible she might live.

Everything in the house was a perfect reproduction of her family home, alike enough to have been the actual house. As she walked from room to room, alternately calling for her sister, brother and parents, Hector, her pet cat, began following her. Relieved at his company, she knelt down and stroked his head. He purred under her touch. It seemed so natural to bend down, but it had been a long time since she'd been able to move. Luxuriating in her actions, she ran her hand over his body. Hector had been dead for at least ten years. She'd been devastated at the time. Nothing was clear to her about how she came to be in the house or why. She had no memory of entering. Calling for her family was a vain hope; she knew she was alone. They were not dead.

Adelaide had spent the week following her consultant's appointment panicking – crying and screaming as if the pain were physical. Unable to calm herself, she'd stand in the kitchen attempting to draw breath and clasping onto her sister's arms to steady herself. She couldn't be alone. Alarmed at her behaviour, Imogen tried to soothe her.

"They have to tell you the worst-case scenario, Ade, to be sure, to cover themselves." Adelaide shook her head with frantic movements, denying that was the case.

"You were there, you saw how serious she was." And the panic would start again, with Adelaide repeating, "I can't believe it, I can't believe it, I can't believe it."

She couldn't eat for fear that being unable to swallow would confirm the diagnosis. At night she clung onto Simon, crying as he reassured her.

"Let's just take one day at a time."

He'd lure her to sleep only for her to jolt awake at the remembrance of her situation, and she would cry again. This process continued for weeks, until the idea of dying settled on her like a toxic dust. Death became part of her normal, everyday thoughts and panic was reduced to regular intervals.

Although the house was her family home, it contained none of the paraphernalia of human life. It was unnaturally clean. Every surface was clear, the usual piles of paperwork were absent and the jumbled drawers of junk collected as "things we might need in the future" were tidy. No shoes loitered at the bottom of the stairs. It was like a show home. Her bedroom still had the bunk beds she had shared with Imogen, but the top bed was made with such precision not a crease was visible on the duvet. Her cosmetics and toiletries were laid out in rows on her dressing table and her wardrobe was full of clothes that hung one item to a hanger. She sat on her bed and beckoned Hector to come and sit with her. When she'd shared a room with her sister she'd tried any amount of nagging, violence or bribery to get Imogen to leave her things as she'd wanted them, but now the neatness felt cold. Her sister should bounce through the door, climb onto her bed and demand to wear Adelaide's new top just because she felt entitled to it.

At work her boss hadn't been especially sympathetic, at least not in the beginning. If she needed time off for appointments she was expected to work extra hours and make up the time. But then she hadn't actually told her boss how serious things were. Adelaide had worked in her local library for eight years. As a sixth former she'd completed her two weeks' work experience at the British Library, and decided that's what she wanted to do. Following an obvious path as an undergraduate, she studied English literature and history, and then went on to complete a master's degree in library studies. At some point her plan to work at the British Library, or in a specialist collection, subsided and she accepted that one's desires didn't always come to fruition. After her initial ambition faded, working in the local library satisfied her. It wasn't exactly exciting but she believed that she had a moderate amount of talent and intelligence and that was reflected in her situation. She was content to organise local book groups and help individuals with their information needs. Until now. Looking to her past gave her a feeling of vertigo: she'd wasted so much time. Questioning every choice she'd made throughout her life, she regretted settling for what had come easily. She'd failed to seize opportunities for excitement, pleasure and advancement.

Her decision not to share her health issues at this stage was a practical one. There was little point in discussing it and making false claims before she was fully diagnosed.

Adelaide made one exception. She'd been friends with Bret for five years, ever since he'd come to work at the library. Mostly they laughed together, sharing an almost puerile sense of humour, and she'd told him without reserve details about her life. They had a casual intimacy. He sometimes had strange beliefs, and Adelaide suspected he had a secret sadness he couldn't confess. To counter this, he'd follow whatever self-help or spiritual trend was in fashion. His current fad was Kabbalah.

"Honestly, Ade, I've met people whose lives have been totally transformed after they start going to the meetings. It's a great focus." His enthusiasm never failed, no matter how many times he started over with a new belief. This one even had an answer to her problem. "There was a man who had stomach cancer; he joined Kabbalah and stayed up all night meditating with his group. By the morning he was cured." This was incredible, even by Bret's standards.

"So you're suggesting if I meditate all night I'll cure my nerve damage?"

"It's worth a go." He shrugged.

"You do realise how serious nerve damage is?"

"So is cancer. Can't make it any worse. Come along to a meeting." Adelaide couldn't handle Bret's illogical, blind belief, and that desperate people were taken in by such ideas made her furious. Her initial instinct to keep her condition to herself had been right.

The fridge was full of all her family favourites, even the German frankfurters that her brother loved. She broke off the end of one of the sausages and put it in her mouth. It tasted exactly as it should. At least she wouldn't go hungry, but then she didn't even know if she could go hungry. She turned on the tap and the water flowed. Outside the window the street was quiet. Cars lined up on either side of the road and a dog barked in the distance. Light streamed through the window of the front door, diffused by a net curtain. She tried the door handle, the door wouldn't move. Checking the lock, she turned the key back and forth, but whichever way it was positioned made no difference; the door stayed shut.

Twisting the key on the back door, she pulled it

open and stepped into the garden. Her panic abated; she wasn't trapped. Hector trotted onto the grass and laid down, his legs sprawled in all directions and his furry stomach upturned to the air. Adelaide knelt on the grass beside him, relieved she could escape, and rubbed his stomach with pleasure. Leaning back onto the grass, she watched the roofs of the houses as they peered over the top of the fence, and then closed her eyes. She had missed this. When she'd lived at home she'd loved to watch Hector lounging on the grass, enjoying the heat of the sun. After a few minutes she got up and went to the back gate. They rarely used it, so she expected it to be stiff. She pulled on the iron bolt: it wouldn't budge. She tried again, but still it didn't move. Appeasing herself, she reasoned it was okay, the fence wasn't high; she could climb over it. Putting a garden chair in front of the gate, she stepped onto it. Reaching up to the top of the fence, she tried to grab it, but couldn't get an adequate grip. Frustrated, she tried again: it slipped from her grasp. This was incredible; as a teenager, she'd been an accomplished climber. When she'd forgotten her keys she could get up onto the front porch, climb the drainpipe and wiggle through the bathroom window. Breathing deep to keep calm, she forced her hands forward to the fence. Still the grip evaded her. Exhausted she jumped down from the chair. Adelaide cried. She couldn't understand what this place was or what she was expected to do here.

There was not – in fact – a single test that could confirm a diagnosis, which meant Adelaide had to undergo a series of procedures. A picture of her symptoms would then be compiled and the consultant would make an assessment.

During this time, Imogen made the announcement she was pregnant. She'd been trying for the last two years and had suffered three miscarriages. Imogen had cried to Adelaide, frightened she'd never be able to have a child. But Adelaide had reassured her that it would just be a matter of time and that it wasn't unusual for women to miscarry before being able to conceive. She'd read that it happened to a third of women. Imogen had waited over four months before telling anyone, even Adelaide, for fear of miscarrying a fourth time.

The radio blurted "his death was a mystery". "Death" was the word her mind picked out as the sound of the machine started up. Together the radio and machine created a discordant cacophony. *Pissh, comm, pissh, comm, pissh, comm.* The machine sounded like an electronic imitation of a steam engine. It was overwhelming. Being physically constrained and trapped, coupled with the intense noise, frightened her. Her head was held in place by a brace. Banging surrounded her. It continued in a regular rhythm as if someone with a hammer was desperate to break in. Without notice, the banging changed to a screech. The mechanical beast was in pain. On occasion the bed would jolt forward and readjust for the next round of images. The interior entombed her, the top lingering only a few inches away from her face. Adelaide closed her eyes and recited the C scale. And then recited it again. Repeating it kept the panic at bay. She'd been learning the piano for just over a year and had recently taken her Grade 1 exam. Being able to play an instrument had been one of her ambitions since childhood. Although she'd tried a few times it had never stuck. At last she was making progress and could see a time when she'd be able to play well. She loved it; proud of what she'd achieved. But it had been her music teacher who had pointed out her fingers hadn't strengthened; in fact, her thumbs were getting weaker. Unable to face giving up, she'd kept going as long as her fingers had allowed. She was to have three scans, each taking twenty minutes. Keeping her eyes tight shut she continued reciting her scales and blocking out the cycle of changing sounds, each more alarming than the last.

"It's perfect, Adelaide." Imogen was staring at the screen. Adelaide was surprised at how well formed the baby was. Each part of it was clearly definable. She'd had no idea that babies were so well developed at twenty weeks of growth. The black-and-white screen illuminated Imogen and Jack's beaming faces.

"Would you like to know the sex?" the sonographer asked. Imogen laughed.

"You have to keep it secret, Ade."

"Of course, what do you take me for?" Adelaide pretended to be offended. The sonographer pushed the probe over her sister's protruding belly. They all stared at the screen.

"The baby's got its leg in the way. Sorry, I can't see." Imogen lightly tapped her stomach and the baby shifted its position. "You've got it trained already." The sonographer laughed as she repositioned the probe. After a pause she announced, "It's a girl. There" She pointed to the screen. "You can you see the vagina." Imogen was grinning.

"Wonderful." She kissed Jack. "I've always wanted a girl."

Adelaide hadn't even thought about wanting a baby. She was thirty-three and had imagined there'd be plenty of time to consider having a family. Her sister was creating life and hers might be coming to an end. For the first time, she felt dislocated from Imogen.

Trapped in the house but no longer trapped in her body, Adelaide ran around, relishing every step. Forgetting things on purpose gave her an excuse to run upstairs and fetch them. And bathing everyday meant she could enjoy climbing in and out of the bath. Initially, she was unsure of how her body would function, but during the first few days it became obvious she still became hungry and tired in the same way. When she was alive and in full health she'd cycled everywhere. Sometimes she felt like the perfect stereotype of a librarian, slowly cycling to and from work, taking things at her own pace. Her bicycle had a traditional frame in a beautiful deep green. It was the freedom and independence that cycling gave her that she most enjoyed. By the power of her own body, she could get to where she needed to go, never having to wait for public transport. She'd only given up when she could no longer lift her leg high enough to step over the frame.

Unable to leave the house, she obviously couldn't cycle, but she could roller-skate. The Christmas before Adelaide left home, Imogen had bought her a pair of rainbow-coloured roller boots. They had bright red wheels and she'd chosen them because they resembled a pair she'd owned as a child. It was their joint plan to resurrect a much-loved hobby. However, on their first outing Adelaide, attempting to show off, had skated backwards around a bend at high speed, lost her footing and crashed into a stationary car, knocking herself out. After that the skates had been dumped in the cupboard under the stairs and left for dead.

The skates were still there. Adelaide took a risk that the neighbours couldn't leave their houses either and turned up the stereo as loud as it would go. The laminate flooring was the ideal surface for a roller disco. At first she wobbled and held onto the dining chairs, but soon she was able to cross the room, and by the end of the third song she considered herself a resurrected dancing queen. She laughed aloud, dancing and spinning.

"The skates aren't wasted now, Imogen." She stopped and looked around the room at the door, half hoping Imogen would walk through it. She turned off the music. The house was silent.

The refuge of expecting the worst wasn't enough to keep her safe. Hope, fragmented and transitory, kept breaking into her thoughts. Hundreds of times she entered her symptoms into the search engine and trawled the results for any condition that contradicted the current theory. She searched until she found a benign explanation. This gave her a respite. Once again she had a future, again the luxury of

SARAH GRAY

wasting time and basking in the feeling that life could be taken for granted. In these periods, the thought that she was having tests was a comfort. At the least, it meant that there was reasonable doubt she wasn't dying.

One evening, after her regular choir practice, her toes clipped the edge of a raised cobblestone and she fell in the middle of the road in front of a busy theatre. The crowd queuing up for the performance stared at her. People were confused when she called for help. Adelaide was scared the lights would change and the traffic begin to flow. A couple in smart business clothes stepped forward.

"Are you hurt?" the woman asked. They both looked worried for her.

"I can't get up. I can't get up. I don't have the strength." Increasing panic intensified her voice. As the man attempted to pull her from the ground, he was surprised at encountering her dead weight. Adelaide clung to him as he lifted her, her face pushing against his chest and her legs limp. She smelled his mix of sweat and cologne. The woman stared at them, frowning as she watched their awkward wrestling. She clutched at Adelaide's bag. When Adelaide was on her feet, she was embarrassed. "So sorry. Sorry, thank you, thank you." Retrieving her bag from the woman, she continued to apologise and limped to the side of the road. The couple stared after her.

"Are you sure you're okay? Is there anything we can do?" Adelaide didn't want to cry in front of them.

"No, thank you, I'm fine, honestly. Thank you." She walked with slow deliberate steps and, as she turned the corner, allowed herself to cry. Shocked and hurt, she limped towards the bus stop. Her knee had been twisted and the skin on her hand was broken and bloody. But it was the realisation of how vulnerable she had become that terrified her.

Once again, the skates were enshrined under the stairs. The novelty of being able to move again had begun to wane; not that she wasn't pleased, but it was becoming normal. Distraction techniques were something she'd have to develop but at least she had plenty to do. The TV worked, there was a vast DVD collection and loads of books. Books had been a central part of her life and her parents had allowed her to create a library in the living room. She suspected her dad secretly passed the books off as his own to make himself look educated. Both of her parents worked in office jobs, her father for an insurance firm and her mother at the local council. Neither of them had been to university and as far back as she could remember her father's advice had been to stay at school or college as long as possible. It had less to do with getting an education than work being a lifelong burden.

Photographs of Thomas, Imogen and Adelaide in their graduation gowns all glared down from the shelf. Thomas was four years older than her and had gone off to university when she was in Year 10. Since that time he had hardly spent any time at home. He was either on a work placement abroad or away with friends, and then in his first job he met his girlfriend. During Adelaide's illness he had sent her flowers and the odd text, but she'd only seen him a few times. He was ambitious and self-contained. Once he'd decided on the life he wanted, he fully committed to it with an intensity that Adelaide admired. He'd had his own company by the time he was twenty-six and travelled all over the world. The rest of the family, no longer a crucial part of his existence, joked he must have been switched at birth. She envied his direction and drive, wishing she had been equally ambitious.

Scanning the shelves, she looked for books she hadn't read. They were usually the long, challenging classics, which would take time and fortitude to finish: *Don Quixote*, *David Copperfield* and *War and Peace*. She now had plenty of time. Pulling *War and Peace* from the shelf, she flicked through it. The pages were bare. She checked *Don Quixote*; again, the pages were empty. Frantic, Adelaide fumbled through the pages of *Vanity Fair*. This was one of her favourite novels; the pages were intact. Working along the shelves, Adelaide looked through the pages of every book. All of the books she hadn't read had blank pages.

Slumped on the sofa, Adelaide turned on the television. She pressed play on the remote and waited for the DVD to work. Again, any film she hadn't seen produced a fuzzy black-and-white screen. Flicking through the channels was a futile act; she knew that anything she could watch she would already have seen. Adelaide was stuck in a world of repeats and rereads. Hector jumped up and snuggled next to her, watching as she ate her ever-replenishing supply of hot dogs. She offered him a piece, but he sniffed it and left it uneaten on the cushion. There was some consolation in her comfort food and Hector's adoration. But this odd half life had no explanation or logic.

When she woke up a youth panel show was blaring out from the television; young, attractive people mocked each other about their choice of funny videos picked from YouTube. She remembered having seen this when she'd been staying in a hotel alone. Nervous at sleeping away from home, she'd kept the TV on all night. Blue light from the screen flickered and it was cold. Hector had moved onto her lap to keep warm. Her feet were freezing and she noticed a strong breeze coming from the hallway. Removing Hector, she leaned forward to see where the draft could be coming from. The front door was wide open.

Adelaide was intrigued at the variety of tests she had to go through. After the claustrophobia of the MRI scan came a lumber puncture. The information leaflet made it sound gruesome. A local anaesthetic would be administered to the lower back and then a needle inserted into the spine and fluid extracted. Adelaide wasn't afraid of needles in particular, but the idea of having her spine tampered with made her uncomfortable. In the waiting room she looked at the other people there and wondered what might be wrong with them. There was an elderly couple and the woman looked frail, with her bony fingers and ghoulishly translucent skin. An engagement ring, heavy with a large diamond, hung limp and loose on her left hand. She clung onto a folder that was full of what looked to Adelaide like appointment letters. A middle-aged man, plump in the face and round-bellied, flicked through a lifestyle magazine. On the television a quizmaster asked quick-fire questions.

Adelaide tried to answer and the plump-faced man joined in, and they laughed when they answered a question wrong. After the quiz show, a couple were shown around country homes to see if any met their ideal of rural living. Everything appeared to be so normal. She must appear normal to those she shared the waiting room with. After forty minutes, Adelaide was invited into a treatment room. The doctor carried her bag as he apologised for the late running of the clinic.

"It's been mad here this morning," he told them. Adelaide was convinced he'd carried the bag because he knew how bad things were for her.

"Just take your shoes off, loosen your clothes so I can get access to your lower back, and pop yourself up here on the bed." He had dark curls and spoke in a gentle voice. The light was too bright, making everything look harsh and stark.

"The procedure sounds worse than it is. The anaesthetic is the most painful part." It stung, but that only lasted a few moments. "It won't take long to feel the effect. Lie still, I'll be back in a minute." She was lying on her side in a foetal position. Simon sat in front of her, holding her hand.

"Don't worry, it will be over soon." He kissed her cheek. The rest of the procedure was easy. She couldn't see what the doctor was doing and couldn't feel it.

"Over. I told you it sounds worse than it is. I just need to get the nurse to do some special bloods that Dr Wells has requested. You need to rest for half an hour anyway; it takes a little while for the spinal fluid to get back to normal." He disappeared through the curtain, taking the sample with him.

"Special bloods. Jesus. What do you think that means?" Adelaide was actually pleased. It might mean that the consultant had thought of some lesser disease, one which might not mean death.

The flat was in a state of disarray and there were half-packed boxes in all of the rooms, except for the kitchen, which had been packed up entirely. Simon and Adelaide had lived in this flat for seven years. She'd loved it, and although it was small, she'd enjoyed making the most of all the space. Wherever a shelf could be built, she'd put one in, and had even designed a perfectly snug work unit and library in the spare room.

In their bedroom, the duvet was crumpled into a ball and sat in the centre of the mattress. The clock showed her the time and date. It had been nearly three months since her death. Time no longer made sense; she'd only been in the house for a week. Simon would be at work now and she longed to see him. Their half-empty home reminded her of when they'd moved in and had expected to spend a lifetime together.

A grey dim light made the living room seem cold. She walked to the window. Rain fell and a large puddle had collected in the gutter directly in front of the building. Standing in the tiny garden there was a "For Sale" sign, but "Sold" blocked out the words. He obviously didn't feel the need to stay in their home to remind him of her and relive memories of their life together. That's what she'd have done. Or maybe he was moving because it was too sad for him to remain. This explanation appeased her, making her still feel loved. But after another moment, anger overwhelmed her. It was so hurtful. He hadn't cared at all. If he had, then he couldn't even think about moving. Moving on.

Adelaide wanted to find him, go to his office and see him, try to ask him if he'd really loved her. But she was in another life where she didn't know the rules. She didn't know if she could see other people, or them her, or if she could travel as normal. There was only one way to find out.

Opening the flat door she walked through the frame. Once again she stood in the hallway of her childhood home. Hector trotted up and sat at her feet.

"Come in, don't be shy. I'm Dr Pym." The consultant neurophysiologist thrust out a rough hand. Adelaide offered hers in return and it was engulfed by a double-handed grasp.

"Ms Anderson, sit on the bed. There are some chairs over there." He indicated to a blue adjustable bed and some plastic chairs. Simon lifted a chair from the pile and placed it next to the bed. On the other side of the room sat a serious-looking young woman. "This is Dr Khan; she's training. You don't mind her sitting in, do you?"

"Of course not, everyone needs to learn." Adelaide smiled at the straight-faced trainee doctor. She nodded back in acknowledgment.

"Okay, so what have we got here today?" Dr Pym was pawing through her medical notes. Adelaide was aghast that he didn't already know. But then decided that it was a good sign; she was low priority, of lesser importance, not needing the attention of a busy consultant. It was all good. He spent a few moments turning pages back and forth and making the occasional grunt. He addressed Dr Khan. "Seems distal at the moment." Again Dr Khan nodded and then got up and stood in front of Adelaide.

"Do you mind?" She asked Dr Pym, not Adelaide.

"Not at all. Go ahead."

"Lift up your arm." Dr Khan began to perform the standard neurological tests. By this time Adelaide knew the tests well, but she would have preferred it if Dr Khan had asked her. She felt like public property. Being ill seemed to mean anyone could invade your personal space. The intrusion of the trainee had been too spontaneously assertive and it unbalanced Adelaide's notion of how an appointment should proceed.

"It's not the tests I'm afraid of, it's the results." Adelaide forced a laugh.

Dr Khan pushed down flat on Adelaide's elevated elbow; it gave way and settled about halfway between her shoulder and side.

"Three." Moving to her hands, she interlocked their fingers. "Grip as hard as you can." Adelaide complied.

"Four. Now pull up as hard as you can." Dr Khan had her wrist against Adelaide's. She pulled. "Three."

"Okay. Thank you, good work." Dr Pym flipped through the file one more time. Looking at the file pages, he commented to no one in particular, "Looks like Dr Wells has some ideas about your diagnosis. Not very optimistic, but then anyone who ends up at her clinic knows the outlook's bad."

Stunned by the truth presented with such casual brutality, Adelaide sat there, silent.

Imogen and Elinor sat at the dining room table having lunch. Elinor had two bear-shaped snacks and they were chatting, giving Imogen a performance. Adelaide stood watching them, transfixed. A relief that she had never felt before lightened her body, as if she were in love. She laughed as Elinor bit the head off one of the bears. They all laughed and for a moment Adelaide felt they were all sharing the joke together. Normality had been restored. The dining room was as she remembered it. The shelf full of miniature flamingoes was a shock of pink. Imogen had a lifelong fondness for flamingoes. The doorbell rang.

"Come in. It's just through the living room." Imogen followed the collection driver and his assistant. Adelaide was sitting in Imogen's chair next to Elinor. They watched as Imogen led the men, or rather the man and his teenage companion, who looked as if he wouldn't be able to lift a dustpan and brush, through to the extension. The extension had been built to accommodate Adelaide when she'd been too weak to manage. Simon had agreed that she should move out of their flat and into Imogen's house. He had kind of moved in, living out of his suitcase, his clean laundry dumped in one corner of the room, his dirty laundry in the other.

She wasn't sure how she'd feel at seeing the room again and followed Imogen with caution. Her first impression was how light it was. The far wall, which led out onto the garden, was entirely glass. She remembered how she'd loved watching the birds come and go. It had kept her amused for hours. At dusk, she'd been lulled to sleep by the rhythmic cooing of the wood pigeons. The men worked with speed, disassembling her bed.

Simon had hardly shown his emotions throughout her illness, but one evening he'd sat on the edge of her bed, feeding her dinner, and she'd commented that it wasn't the worst thing, being looked after.

"No, being without you is the worst thing. A hundred years with you wouldn't be enough." Then he'd cried and hugged her tight. But within two minutes he'd dried his eyes and continued feeding her.

There was already a piano in the room. It had been the plan to make it into a music room. There was a picture of her and Imogen on the top of it. They were wearing their glad rags and most glamorous make-up. It had been taken at their cousin's wedding and they were hugging, their cheeks pushed together. They looked happy. Adelaide couldn't believe this had been taken only a year before she'd become ill. She laid her fingers on the keys; she longed to play. She'd thought she'd be a role model to Elinor, encouraging her in her musical endeavours, and had imagined playing duets together. She'd also thought they'd have sleepovers and go to the seaside.

At least she could spend time with her now, even if Elinor wasn't aware of it.

Adelaide followed the teenager as he clung onto the back end of the mattress and edged it through into the living room. Elinor had finished her lunch and was forcing her feet into a pair of wellies. Imogen returned from showing the removers out. She wiped tears from her eyes and blew her nose.

"Now that's all over we can get on with things again. Do you want to help Mummy with some gardening?" Elinor nodded her head up and down. Imogen pulled back the patio door and Elinor ran out into the garden. It was a joy to see her. Adelaide followed Imogen through the garden door and was again back in the hallway of her old home.

Now that the diagnosis was official it was as if she was being initiated into a secret club. In one morning she saw a physiotherapist, a wheelchair occupational therapist, met the clinic secretary and had a consultation with a specialist nurse.

"Most people are just relieved to know what's wrong with them," one of them said in a professionally caring tone. If she'd just been told she had an overactive thyroid or a broken leg she would be inclined to agree. But to be told at thirty-three that she had a massively reduced life span didn't coincide with what she considered a relief.

It was also hard to remember she wouldn't die as she was. Although weak, she could still walk, stand up with a struggle and climb stairs, albeit slowly. If she could halt the disease at this point she'd cope. Disability was preferable to death. Adelaide was pacified by the idea that at the time of her death, she'd be so fed up with being ill, she'd be happy to die. However, it abhorred her to imagine that anyone would say, "It's better she's gone and out of her misery". It would be better not to have been ill at all. Obviously.

Everything about life had changed. Her assumptions about her future had been destroyed. Gone was the "positive illusion" of a predictable and controllable world. She'd never get old and her parents would outlive her. Nothing made sense. People around her looked alien, were alien. Their experience no longer coincided with hers and she felt outside of everyday pleasures, ordinary worries and trivial concerns.

Adelaide was frightened to be alone but alienated from people who didn't know what was happening to her. It was difficult to chat about holidays and future plans, while keeping the abyss that faced her a secret. When she did confide in others she found she continued to be lonely. People didn't find it easy to hang out with someone who has just told them they are going to die. Plus, it was difficult to cope with their reactions. Some people became upset, and some who wouldn't cry if she'd died, cried to hear she was going to die. Of course, Adelaide was aware they were crying partly for the shadow cast over their own mortality, but she kept quiet, watching the security of their lives crumble.

More people than Adelaide would have guessed reacted by underplaying her illness. Some said, "Well, we've all got to die sometime"; others, "None of us know how long we have"; and the most clichéd, "I could get run over by a bus tomorrow". Confused and angered, she'd often reply that she could see her bus coming up the road and couldn't get out of the way, while theirs was still parked at the depot. She never felt guilty about frightening them. It was exactly because their own deaths were abstract that they could say such things.

Adelaide felt that no one should know when they were going to die. Often she'd watch people cross the road, weaving between the cars without concern for their lives. If they were given a terminal diagnosis, they'd be devastated, but without it thought nothing of risking their lives on a daily basis.

Although she didn't want to, Adelaide realised that she would have to take responsibility for how people treated her. If she was upset, she'd explain she didn't need solutions or cheering up, but just wanted some sympathy. If she wanted to express how unfair it was or how grief stricken she was, she didn't need unrealistic optimism, only an acknowledgment of how sad she was. Eventually, she wanted to scream at people not to waste their time and to embrace existence with all their energy. Waiting for the conditions of life to be perfect was pointless; if you couldn't afford ten days in the Bahamas, then a weekend at Camber Sands would be enough.

At work she'd decided to tell her boss the whole story. Her symptoms still weren't obvious and she'd managed to avoid lifting piles of books and using the ladders. She often volunteered to help library users with difficult enquiries so her absences from the physical work weren't too obvious. But she kept crying, unable to contain her grief. At these moments she'd repeat to herself, "I'm going to die". Her colleagues were sure to notice something was wrong.

Donna was sympathetic when she heard the diagnosis. She listened when Adelaide shared her fears and allowed her to talk about her situation over and over, as if talking could make it right again. Adelaide would cry and wasn't ashamed, feeling that Donna had invited her to confide. Donna's own sister had died the previous year. They'd been close and it had taken her three months to get back to work full-time. As assistant manager, it had been Adelaide's job to take responsibility and make sure everything was running smoothly. She'd been happy to do it. To Adelaide, losing her sister was one of the worst things she could imagine. Supporting Donna through her loss was the least she could do. And now Donna was supporting her.

"I'll put you on light duties, but the one thing I ask of you is don't cry in front of the library users. If you're feeling overwhelmed just let me know and we can pull you off the front desk."

Adelaide was grateful. She wanted to stay at work as long as possible. Being home alone would be unbearable, giving her too much time to think about her situation.

Bret's unsympathetic reaction to her potential diagnosis had meant she'd avoided him as much as possible but now she missed him and felt sure that her certain death would have some impact.

"Healing works on an emotional and spiritual level, Ade. I know it's not popular to say but people with chronic illness have closed down on life." He crunched on a raw carrot.

"So you think I don't want to live enough, that's why I'm ill?" Adelaide could hardly believe anyone, much less a friend, could be so cruel.

"Through Kabbalah, I've met some fantastic

people, they're so high on life they never get sick. Believe me Ade, not even a cold."

Adelaide couldn't speak.

"Until we're on their spiritual level there'll always be hospitals and treatments for the rest of us. I'd better get back, Donna's in a mood today." He snapped his lunchbox closed and left the room. Adelaide felt winded. Donna entered the staff room.

"It's been a hell of a morning." She plopped a tea bag into a mug and flicked on the kettle. She turned to Adelaide. Adelaide tried to smile. "Are you crying? Again."

"I'm sorry, it was Bret ..." Donna stopped her.

"Listen Ade, you have to decide if you can cope at work. If you can't hold it together, then you need to think about leaving."

So she left. Everything had changed and pretending it hadn't, that everything was normal, that she was just like Bret (only on a lower plane of existence) was not possible, not on any level.

The library was quiet, which was normal for the mid-afternoon slump. Donna was at the desk, tidying up, attempting to look busy. One of the assistants was reshelving books; she couldn't see who it was but could hear the muffled sound of books being shuffled and inserted on the shelf. Walking amongst the aisles she inhaled the smell and ran her hand over the rows of books. She loved the library; it had been a safe place.

Bret's voice carried across the room.

"Come on, ladies. Welcome. Sit down." The snug was set amongst the main fiction section and she could just see Bret sitting on one of the comfy chairs within a closed circle. It was the book club. Adelaide wondered if Bret was the regular group leader now. For a brief moment she experienced a surge of jealousy. Sitting in an empty chair, she decided she would join the group. She didn't have anything better to do.

At five past the hour, Bret began. "So, ladies …" A dapper chap cleared his throat. Bret laughed. "And of course, gentleman." The women giggled. It was obvious Bret was good at this. People loved him and she had too – except for his clutching at a merry-go-round of spiritual beliefs. The book club had been her responsibility and she was ashamed to admit to herself that she'd made sure of it. Bret wouldn't have had a chance when she was alive.

Adelaide had worked out that when in the land of the living she was trapped wherever she arrived. She had no control over where the open door sent her. Going through an exterior door led her back to her family house; it was a closed cycle. She longed to see Simon, but would have to wait until the door led her to him. After the book club, she couldn't bear to leave. Even if no one could hear or see her it was revitalising for her to be around people. Deciding to stay until closing time, she followed Bret on his duties. It would be just like being at work. Chattering on, she talked at Bret, recounting shared experiences or telling him about her new life, trying to make sense of it.

"I don't even know how it's decided where I go when I walk through the front door. Why am I at the library today but not yesterday? I'm just here. Isn't that crazy?" By the end of the day, she was fed up with talking to herself.

The dusk was beautiful. One of the features of the library that made it so special was its combination of old stone and glass. From the main desk the local park could be seen, and the evening light reflected gold into the building.

"The library will be closing in fifteen minutes. Please check out your books at the front desk in the next five minutes." Donna loved making announcements. As the last users left the building Bret stood near to Donna, hovering. "Go on then, get lost."

He grabbed his coat and bag from behind the service desk and was gone within thirty seconds, waving as he went. Adelaide wished she could go with him.

It had been important to Adelaide to know her life meant something to Simon and Imogen, as if love was a consolation. She kept asking them, "Do you love me?", "Will you miss me when I'm gone?". "You won't forget me, will you?" If she was loved then her life hadn't been wasted. Imogen was matter-of-fact.

"Of course I love you, don't be silly."

All the time, Simon told her he loved her but wouldn't entertain talk of a time when Adelaide would be gone.

"No one is dying today or tomorrow. I'm not thinking beyond that. Let's just keep going and in thirty years we'll look back having spent a lifetime together." It infuriated and comforted her in equal measures. She needed him to be realistic about their situation to express her grief, but his denial blocked her. However, his talent to compartmentalise helped her to contain her sadness and live in the moment. And that was a small gift. Having so few moments left, she was trying not to squander them on grief and anger. When she told him this, she joked she'd have time for that when she dead.

Three weeks after the diagnosis was finally confirmed, Imogen went into labour. Adelaide stood at the bottom of the bed peering over Imogen's raised feet. She'd been having contractions for some hours, with little progress, but Adelaide and

Jack had refused to leave. The nurse warned them it could be a long wait but they still insisted. When the time came to actually push, Adelaide was scared for Imogen. Childbirth was dangerous. There were no guarantees it would end happily. She wanted the baby but her priority was Imogen.

"The epidural isn't working, it hurts." Imogen raised her voice.

"It's okay, you're doing fine. Just keep calm ..."

Imogen shouted. "For fuck's sake, how can I keep calm when I feel like I'm splitting open?" Jack was holding onto her hand and kissed her head. Imogen shooed him away.

"Get off. I can't breathe with you all over me."

He stepped back and looked at the midwife, searching for an explanation. The midwife smiled at him.

"It's okay, we usually hear much worse."

Adelaide stood back from the scene. Staring from Imogen to the machine that monitored the baby's heart-rate, she expected it to stop at any moment.

"Keep going, breathe, wait for the contraction, and then push." Imogen screamed.

After Imogen had been pushing for nearly three hours the midwife told her to stop.

"The baby is twisted and the shoulders are stuck. Don't worry, the baby's heart-rate is fine, it's not in distress, but I am going to ask the paediatrician to help. If you agree."

"I don't have much choice." Imogen was exhausted. The midwife spoke to her trainee.

"Can you go and tell Sister that we need Dr Patel's assistance in Suite 5. Thanks, Gem."

Adelaide panicked. Imogen had had her legs in the air for hours and the baby was stuck. She understood now why bringing life into the world was so dangerous. The midwife remained calm. "I'll show you." She pushed her hands into Imogen's vagina and pulled it apart to reveal the dark hairy head of the baby. Jack smiled. "You've certainly got a hairy one," the midwife laughed.

Adelaide was overwhelmed: simultaneously disturbed and amazed. It was incredible how the vagina changed and mutated to provide the appropriate canal for the birth. The human body was amazing – except hers. Hers had turned against her. It had given up without her permission.

Within minutes of the paediatrician being in the room, she had decided Imogen would have to go to theatre. And within another few minutes Imogen had been wheeled away, Jack following in gown and gloves. Adelaide waited alone in the delivery suite. Steeped in worries of what could go wrong, she watched the clock and stepped through what she imagined was happening in the operating theatre.

The baby was twisted; maybe forceps would be used to tease it out, or the ventouse would drag the baby into the world – instruments and techniques seemingly designed for medieval torture. If Imogen or the baby became distressed there would have to be an emergency C-section. Adelaide couldn't help her thoughts sliding into disaster. Jack might come back holding a baby but crying, explaining that Imogen hadn't made it. Half an hour had passed and Adelaide was frantic. She was sure either one or both of them were dead.

The midwife wheeled in a transparent cot and parked it next to her.

"Imogen – is she alright?" Adelaide was exhausted with nerves.

"No need to look so worried, she's in the recovery room. They'll bring her through in a little while. Aren't you interested in your baby niece?" Adelaide looked into the cot. "I'll leave you two together."

The midwife left the room and Adelaide was alone with the baby. Wrapped tight in a blanket, her eyes closed, she was perfect, with her wrinkled, red face. To Adelaide, she looked like a tiny pixie on loan from the spirit world. She wanted to stroke her face, but refrained for fear of harming her or infecting her with human concerns.

"Hello little baby," she said, and the baby opened her eyes. Adelaide was ecstatic; the baby could hear her. They were aware of one another. In that instant, Adelaide fell in love with her sister's baby. Immediately and without conditions and in every way, until the end of time.

Then Adelaide remembered she'd never see her grow up. The baby would never know her.

"My baby has a baby. Let me see her."

Imogen handed her baby over to their mother.

"She is adorable. Well done, sweetheart." Their mother stared down, grinning at the child, and their father peered over her shoulder.

"She looks just like me."

"No, she doesn't look like a gnarly old gargoyle like you." They both laughed. Her father came over and kissed Adelaide on the cheek and gave her an encouraging squeeze on the arm. He'd never kissed her before her diagnosis. This was his way of communicating his support. They never spoke about it, but she sometimes caught him staring at her with a sad, hangdog expression. It almost made her feel sorry for him. But since the baby had been born a day ago, her fury had increased. Her parents were both in their mid sixties; they'd lived a good life. Looking around the ward, she watched doting grandparents. Some were sprightly and smart, active if grey-haired; others shuffled up the ward, unable to move without help. She belonged to the latter group, only thirty-five years too early. Jealous of pensioners, she raged against the loss of her old age. "Hexed" was the word that came to her. What terrible thing had she done to deserve being damned in such a way?

All of the ghost stories she'd read had been wrong. There seemed no way to make people see you when you were dead. Adelaide waited outside Simon's workplace, staring up at the building. A routine when alive, every Tuesday night she'd meet him from work and they'd go for a meal together as a treat to break up the working week. Tuesdays had been her short day. But now, Adelaide couldn't go into the building; walking over the threshold would take her back to her family house. Replicating her past habit, she waved at Simon through the office's plate glass window. Only this time, he didn't hold up his hand to indicate he'd be five minutes. It still gave her pleasure to watch him as he packed his things away for the day, his movements familiar and dear. She kept waiting for him to lift his head and search for her as he had in the past. But he was oblivious to her presence. She was invisible.

Keeping up with Simon's pace was tricky; he was tall and had a long stride. To her advantage she was able to dart through the crowd, creating her own pathway. Desperate not to lose sight of him, she broke into a partial run. It was cruel she'd been dumped in the street. As soon as he went into a building, her way would be blocked; locked as she was in her cycle of purgatory. When Simon turned each corner she imagined holding his hand, and running slightly to keep up with him as she had so many times before. They'd chat about their day and choose what they wanted to eat, their conversation full of the excitement of having completed a day's work and looking forward to the evening ahead. As he entered the pub she stopped and watched him through the glass wall. His back was resolutely to her, standing stiff and unbending at the bar. He looked grimly alone, as if he was suffering from an invisible disease of his own. And she couldn't comfort him. She couldn't even go to him. She prayed for him to get a window seat. A light rain drizzled, creating a grey mist, which hung over the river. Haunting wasn't as she'd thought it would be, not at all.

She wasn't scared of dying, she just wanted more life. The only thing that terrified her was the idea of her dead body being alone in the mortuary. Being locked into a stainless-steel cell seemed so lonely. Her body was gradually weakening and as time passed she would notice, almost by accident, with a casualness that belied her emotions, something she could no longer do: bending down; picking something up; removing a jar lid. It was the small inconveniences that catalogued her decline.

The first time she couldn't get up from the sofa was alarming. Adelaide sat watching Elinor play. Sitting on the floor, surrounded by toys, she grabbed at a small blue elephant just beyond her grasp. It gave Adelaide pleasure to watch her and she couldn't help grinning. Elinor's expression was one of intense concentration as she focused on the elephant. Her small, plump fingers touched the edge of an ear. Unable to grasp it, she pushed forward a little harder until she rocked onto all fours.

"Imogen, come and see. I think Nell is going to crawl." Adelaide shouted. No response. Adelaide tried to stand, using her usual method of placing her hands on the sofa either side of her hips and rocking forward. She couldn't get the momentum she needed to stand. She rested and tried again; she failed.

This was a pattern she came to recognise. She would learn to live with her various disabilities and cope well. It was okay. And then something would change without her having realised it. Halfway to the bus stop she couldn't go on, her legs were heavy and she shuffled, unable to lift her feet high enough to clear the ground.

"Are you sure? Can't you try?" Simon urged her.

"I am trying, what do you think I'm doing? I need the wheelchair." She hobbled towards a wall and rested against it. "I'll wait here."

"But you were walking before." Simon was exasperated.

"Now I'm not. Please Simon. It's hard enough without an argument."

Before she became ill, the idea of being a wheelchair user would have been abhorrent to Adelaide, but now it was a relief. Putting it off, she struggled to walk, convincing herself she was coping just fine. She hadn't fully understood that it was there to help her live as normally as possible, and because she waited until it was out of dire necessity, the transition was a little easier.

Her relief, however, was followed by an inevitable period of adjustment. People stared. She was young; she must be a curiosity. People carried the same look; at first puzzled and then embarrassed as they lowered their eyes. This never varied, whether the individual was young or old, male or female.

Being pushed around was frustrating and sometimes frightening. In the first few days she nearly rolled into the road when Simon stopped to put on his gloves. Turned out there was a reason they'd been told to apply the brakes whenever the wheelchair was stationary. And there were times when Simon overshot and knocked her feet into shop shelving or against doorways. Or when she wanted to look at something specific in a shop she had to explain, "there, no, over there, in front of the birthday cards, there". It was freezing in the chair; even a slight breeze was uncomfortable. Returning from outings in the middle of winter, it would take her hours to warm up and she'd snuggle against Simon until each part of her reached normal body temperature. Her feet rarely did.

Any trip out of the house was a faff. Adelaide needed help with everything. Washing, dressing, putting on her coat, hat and gloves. She still hadn't given up the need to look good and had persuaded Simon, much to his horror, to blow-dry her hair. The result was surprisingly good. Although it wasn't how she would have done it herself, she didn't want to be ungrateful or dissuade him, so tactfully accepted the result. If she was very careful she could still apply make-up. It was slow and not as precise as she'd previously been able to do but she was adamant that even as a curiosity in a wheelchair she could retain some sartorial standards. But everything was a compromise.

When using the bus for the first time, both

Adelaide and Simon were shocked. They were off to Elinor's first birthday party. Simon pushed the button for disabled access. An alarm sounded inside the bus. They waited. Everyone else mooched onto the bus and took their seats. Another alarm went off and the doors shut in front of them. The alarm continued beeping. A ramp slowly emerged from the bottom of the door. The doors reopened.

"The wheelchair area is required, please clear the area. The wheelchair area is required, please clear the area." A young mother with a buggy parked in the wheelchair section began to fold it up. She avoided looking at them. People shuffled down the gangway, attempting to make room. Simon pushed Adelaide into the bus and everyone watched them as he struggled to manoeuvre the chair into the restricted area. A yellow pole blocked the way and Simon had to jerk her into position to get her back against the padded rest. Adelaide cringed. She had become the centre of attention for all the wrong reasons.

Being independent, able-bodied and healthy, had meant that she'd lived half-hidden, taking up as little of life as possible. Increasingly dependent, she was being forced into full sight.

"It's Auntie Adelaide and Uncle Simon." Imogen held the door open and standing behind her was

Elinor, who was holding onto a wooden walker.

"Happy birthday, sweetie. I can't believe she's so confident on her feet." Adelaide laughed at the tiny girl, standing defiant.

"Yes, she can walk really well with the baby-walker." Imogen stroked her small, chestnut head. "Jack, come and help Simon get Ade in please." They lifted her wheelchair over the threshold and Simon pushed her through the house to the back garden. The barbeque smelled delicious and, behind the smoke rising from the coals, her dad raised a kitchen utensil in greeting. Her mum got up from her chair and limped towards her. She bent down and gave her a kiss on the cheek.

"Hello darling, I've been in the wars, as you can see." She indicated her bandaged foot. This was typical of her mother. It was always about her.

"Mum's been trying to DIY again and you know how that usually turns out." Imogen was laughing.

"You cheeky monkey. You're not too big to go over my knee." They were both laughing and Imogen kissed their mother on the head. It made Adelaide angry. Her mother's foot was so trivial and she'd probably brought it on herself. She stared at them both, alienated by their bonhomie.

"You okay, Ade?"

"Fine, thanks." She refused to join in.

"Mum's hurt her foot, Ade. It's not very nice for

her. We were at the hospital most of yesterday afternoon." Adelaide knew what Imogen was trying to say. It wasn't all about her. Life still went on. If they were playing Top Trumps of personal tragedy, she'd be the winner without a doubt, but other people still experienced accidents and pain, relationships failed and jobs were lost. It was churlish of her to undermine the value of other people's problems. Humiliated, Adelaide wanted to cry; Imogen was right.

"Come and show Auntie Adelaide your birthday books. She can read you a story." Imogen suggested in reconciliation. Elinor pushed her walker over to Adelaide and started to unload books onto her lap.

"Which one would you like to read?" Elinor offered up a hard book with a blue truck bulging with animals on the front. "Do you want to come up?" Adelaide held out her hand and Elinor grabbed it. Elinor climbed up and between them they had enough strength to pull her onto Adelaide's lap. Adelaide couldn't run around the garden with her, or get on the floor, but she could read to her.

It was impossible not to get pleasure from being with Elinor. Sitting still on her lap, Elinor was absorbed in the story and occasionally pointed to something in a picture. "That," she said. Adelaide would talk to her about the image. If it was an animal she would make the appropriate noise and Elinor would watch her and sometimes laugh, giggling without restraint. Making Elinor laugh was like winning a prize. When the story was finished, Elinor wriggled down from her lap. She stood for a moment, resting one hand on her knee. Then she stepped forward and walked to Imogen on the other side of the patio. Everyone cheered, clapped and laughed.

"I can't believe she's walking" Imogen laughed with tears in her eyes.

On the way back, the bus was packed. Adelaide sat amongst a group of theatre students, all chatting with zealous enthusiasm about their latest rehearsal.

"I was sooo embarrassed when I slipped," proclaimed a slender boy with a large quiff, which made him appear top heavy.

"Don't worry, dear, I think you got away with it," a young woman answered, her hair also back-combed into an elaborate do. They all loomed over Adelaide, emanating charm and healthy good looks. Occasionally, one of them briefly looked at her and gave her a sympathetic smile. Returning the smile with a forced grin she emphasised her awareness, she couldn't have them thinking she was mentally impaired too.

Adelaide pushed the button to let the driver know she wanted to get off. She couldn't hear the alarm so pushed it again: still there was no sound. Simon was sitting a few rows back and she signalled to him. He shook his head, trying to let her know he didn't understand what she was trying to say. The bus stopped and let passengers off, the doors closed again and the bus started to pull away.

"You've got to press the special button, love," an old woman instructed her. Then an old man next to her started to shout.

"Driver! Driver! Stop! Stop the bus! There's a woman in a wheelchair that wants off!" Simon fought his way towards her.

"Driver! Stop!" the old man continued. At last the bus stopped and the alarm began. Simon managed to get to her.

"Release your brakes." Adelaide took her brakes off and the chair rolled forward into the old woman before Simon had a chance to grab it.

"Simon!" He clasped the chair. "I'm so sorry," Adelaide apologised.

"Don't worry, love." The old woman patted her leg with sympathy. The bus was too packed to let them get out easily. The alarm beeped and the doors drew back. A dozen of the theatre students traipsed off the bus and stood either side of the ramp as if a welcoming committee. Simon wheeled her down the ramp past the students.

"Well, that's the bus then," she said over her

shoulder, making a face at Simon, who shared her mocking grin.

Bret had been right after all. When alive, she hadn't lived fully enough, taken all the opportunities she could have. She'd had her share of life, been found wanting, and so the rest was denied her. The million things she hadn't done haunted her: international travel, adventure, having a baby, her dream of working at the British Library, friends she should have bothered to maintain contact with, those hobbies she'd always intended to pick up. She had let it all slip by.

Not really knowing whom she was addressing, she admitted to some unseen force that she now knew she'd done it wrong, and now she was good, she had changed, she understood what was required of her and could do it better, if she was given the chance to try. She promised.

Adelaide stood on the threshold of the patio door watching her family. Her mother was playing a game of Frisbee with Elinor. Missing the Frisbee, Elinor chased after it as it travelled across the grass. She pretended to trip and rolled behind it, laughing.

"That's enough, darling. Nanny's too hot."

Jack laughed at Elinor's dramatic reaction. "She'll make a great footballer, taking a dive like that." Jack kicked a ball in Elinor's direction. Running after it, she pulled back her small foot and kicked it. It rolled less than a metre. She ran after it again. Adelaide wanted to call to Elinor and join in with the game. As usual, Adelaide's father stood behind the barbeque.

"Two minutes on these burgers." He was poking a patty, squeezing the fat onto the coals. It sizzled. "Delicious." He was pleased with the result.

Imogen walked up behind her, carrying a large bowl of salad, and instinctively Adelaide moved out of her way. Putting the salad on the table, turning, Imogen smiled.

"Listen. Mum, Dad, I'm pregnant." She laughed.

"Oh, my darling, that's wonderful news." Their mother rushed forward, kissed and then hugged her. Imogen was delighted. Adelaide felt sick. Only a few months since she'd died and they didn't seem to care she'd gone at all. Adelaide couldn't watch anymore and stepped over the threshold.

Being dead was complicated. She could move, sort of enjoy day-to-day living, and visit the living world. But she was disconnected from it. Her darling sister was having another baby and didn't appear to show any signs of missing her. Haunting came with too many unexplained restrictions. There were rules she didn't understand and no one to explain them to her. She had no control over where she would end up in the living world; she wanted to see Simon, but the front door rarely delivered her to him. The days passed in a bland routine: getting up, doing a few exercises, reading, watching a film – a repeat – snoozing, having dinner and then more TV. Often, she'd wake up on the sofa having fallen asleep during the evening. Each day was identical to the next. She had no idea when the door would open or where it would lead her.

As usual, she sat on the sofa eating her dinner. Hot dogs again. She put the plate down next to her. There were only so many hot dogs one person could stomach.

"Fancy some hot dog, Hector?" The cat barely twitched. If she could get someone to talk to her, that would make all the difference. It wasn't food that made you alive, it was other people. "What do you think, Hector? Maybe, I could try saying 'BOO!' to people or moving things around like ghosts are supposed to do?" Hector opened his eyes for a moment and then continued snoozing. It was no surprise fictional ghosts were often angry if haunting was so miserable.

When Elinor was out of the house, Adelaide waited for her to return. There were those special days when Elinor would come straight to her, climb on the bed and give her a kiss. Occasionally, when Adelaide had the breath, she read to her. Elinor held the book and turned the pages. They laughed at animal noises, but now Elinor would tell her she was doing it wrong and demonstrate her superior interpretation. When Adelaide couldn't read, her breath shallow and restricted, Imogen would come and sit on the bed and read to them both, Elinor snuggling next to Adelaide, and Adelaide dozing, curled around her niece.

Over the months she'd become tired of being lifted, transferred from bed to wheelchair to commode. Her body ached and she lived in fear of being dropped. It was hard for others to fully understand that, if she fell, it hurt her so much more: her limbs would twist and become trapped under the weight of her immobile body. It was excruciating. Eventually, a hoist was introduced and she barely left her bed. The frustration of being static was one she'd learned to temper. Being left with something just out of reach, or freezing with the window open, or sweating when it was closed, were regular occurrences.

*****

Archie was a beautiful baby, plump and content. Observing his sleeping face was calming. Adelaide sat next to Imogen, smiling to herself as she watched them. Elinor was crouched on the floor sorting the pieces of a jigsaw puzzle.

"Find the edges first, darling," Imogen suggested. She was tired and her hair needed a wash.

"Like this, Mummy?" Elinor held up a piece for Imogen's inspection.

"Does that look like it has a straight side?"

Elinor stared at it and giggled. "It's all wiggly." Elinor was holding up pieces one after another, all with wiggly edges.

"No, that one." Imogen was pointing to an appropriate piece, but Elinor kept picking others.

"Next to it, to the left," Imogen snapped. "No, the left, not the right." Adelaide knelt down beside Elinor and handed her the piece. She hadn't really been meaning to pick something up, but she did. And it was so easy. A wide smile spread across Adelaide's face. But the child took it without reaction.

"This one, Mummy?"

"Yes, at last. Now find the rest." Imogen hadn't noticed. Adelaide continued pushing pieces of the puzzle towards Elinor and they worked together in unacknowledged silence. It only took them a few minutes to assemble the edges of the puzzle. Imogen looked up from Archie. "Wow, Nell – that was quick."

Elinor nodded and smiled, half glancing towards Adelaide. Adelaide wanted to grab her to see if the child really could see her. It did seem as if she was looking at her, but she couldn't be sure.

"Time for bed now, you can finish the rest tomorrow."

Adelaide lay on the sofa and watched the trees being blown by the wind. Lurching shadows reflected against the living room walls. She'd decided not to go back to her halfway house. There was no guarantee when she'd be able to return to the living world and she had to know if Elinor had seen her. She didn't want to scare either Elinor or Imogen but there must be a way of communicating without causing alarm. Her fantasy was all three of them chatting together, sharing a life again. Excitement made her involuntary stand; it might be possible to have a new kind of life.

Running up the stairs, exhilaration still carried her forward. On the landing she slowed and crept towards Imogen's bedroom. The door was open. Adelaide stood at the threshold and watched Imogen and Jack sleeping. Jack was on his back, mouth open, snoring, and Imogen snuggled next to him, curled into a foetal position. Her clenched fists nestled under her chin. She looked cute. Adelaide edged towards the baby's basket. Archie was wriggling his arms and legs as if fighting an imaginary foe. He squeaked and thrashed his head. His mouth opened in prelude to a cry. Imogen stirred. Adelaide withdrew.

A hump of duvet had collected at the head of the bed. A small foot stuck out from the bottom and a mass of hazel hair from the top. The room was beautiful. The shelves were full of books and soft, plush animals, wooden toys and games. Just how she imagined a child's bedroom should be. Cartoon woodland creatures and toadstools covered the soft furnishings. Above the bed hovered large paper orbs in deep pink, bright orange and blue. Adelaide hadn't been upstairs in her sister's house for years. Imogen had consulted her on colours and fabric but once she'd lost her ability to climb stairs she'd been unable to see the final result. Imogen had done a good job. There was a child-sized armchair, again covered with cute fungi. Adelaide would have loved it herself as a child. She pulled it alongside the bed and sat down. Her knees made extreme triangle shapes. Leaning forward she coaxed the duvet away from Elinor's face. The child wriggled. Adelaide froze, but Elinor continued to sleep, her face now peeping out of the duvet. Picking up a book, she opened it, expecting the pages to be bare. But the words were there on the page. The relief of seeing the text felt like breathing new life. So in the living world she could experience new things: it was possible to live again. She began to read, whispering the words.

"Come on, missus, time to get up." Imogen pulled back the bedroom curtains and the light hurt Adelaide's eyes. From the way Elinor hid under the duvet, she was sure the abrupt awakening had been a shock to her too. The book she'd been reading had slipped to the floor. Her neck hurt and was stiff from having hung forward on her chest as she'd slept in the tiny chair.

"Time to get out of bed. School this morning." Elinor sat up. Her hair was matted and she rubbed her eyes. She reminded Adelaide of the pixie she'd seen at birth.

"Red or yellow?" Imogen held up a red cord dress and a pair of yellow, heavy-cotton dungarees. Elinor shook her head.

"No, I want the green one." Elinor was sulking.

"It's in the wash. We'll go with the red." Stamping her feet on the mattress, Elinor cried.

"Not this morning, Elinor, I'm not in the mood." Picking knickers, vest and tights from the draw, Imogen assembled the outfit. This wasn't how Adelaide would wake Elinor. She'd do it gently and give her time. Imogen was being too harsh.

"Now, madam." Elinor slid from the bed and crossed the room. "Arms up." Imogen pulled the pyjama top over Elinor's head and replaced it with a vest.

"Can I have a story?" Elinor asked.

"I don't have time, sweet pea, I've still got to get the baby ready."

Elinor thought for a moment and then said, "What about the lady?" Adelaide couldn't believe it.

"Lady? What do you mean, sweetie? Left foot, please." Imogen wriggled Elinor's foot into the tights.

"The lady that read me a story last night." Elinor held out her right foot.

"Stand up." Imogen pulled up the tights. "You mean Mummy read you a story."

Elinor shook her head. "No, the lady." Elinor's insistence frightened Imogen.

"You're just being silly and playing with Mummy. Come downstairs and get some breakfast." She led Elinor from the room.

Elinor could hear Adelaide. She couldn't leave them now.

Adelaide waited for Imogen to leave Elinor's bedroom. A night-light illuminated the far side of the room and Elinor was snuggled up to her neck under the duvet. As Adelaide walked across the room,

Elinor sat up, listening. Adelaide selected the book from the previous evening. Elinor watched.

"Not that one." Elinor hopped from her bed and ran to the shelf and pulled down a book. She laid it in front of her chair and got back into bed. Adelaide was overwhelmed. Picking up the book, she began to read. Elinor listened, seemingly unconcerned by the strangeness of the situation.

"Can you see all the animals?" Adelaide held the book up. "You used to love the camels. They look so grumpy." Elinor nodded, giggling.

"They're silly." She couldn't stop giggling. Adelaide emulated the camel's expression in the way she would have done when alive. "You look silly too." Adelaide's camel face faded.

"You can see me?" Elinor looked at her and nodded.

"What are you doing still awake?" Imogen stood in the doorway.

"Having a story."

"Well, you should be asleep. You're being too noisy – you'll wake the baby." She bent down and covered Elinor with the duvet and kissed her on the head.

"It's not just me." Elinor sat up again.

"Don't be silly, Nell. Lie down." Elinor refused, stiffening her back in protest.

"It's the lady, she's silly too."

Imogen stood back. "I don't like this, Nell. There's no lady. It's just your imagination." She forced the child down again. "Now, please go to sleep."

Adelaide watched them. She wanted to reassure Imogen it was okay. To wave the book around in her face would be too shocking. Adelaide glanced around the room, looking for a solution. There were some wooden letters on the shelf. She arranged them to spell "Ade". Elinor shouted, pointing.

"Look!" Imogen stared at the letters for a long time. She surveyed the room as if expecting to find someone standing behind her and then turned to Elinor and shouted.

"I've had enough of this! Now get to sleep." She almost ran from the room. Maybe the reason people couldn't see Adelaide was because they couldn't imagine it was possible. Imogen wasn't yet able to believe in her.

Sitting at the piano, Adelaide scrutinised the photograph. Their cousin's wedding had been fun. She'd always had the best of times with Imogen. Although Imogen couldn't see her yet, Adelaide knew it was possible. The house was quiet. Imogen had taken Elinor to reception class and Jack was at work. Placing her fingers on the piano keys, she let them rest. It had been a long time since she'd played. Pressing the keys down, she enjoyed the sound. Running her fingers along the keys, she played a scale and then another and another. It was exhilarating. Sorting through the music books on the rest, she found *Old Time Rags*. She'd loved playing rags. They were joyful and they'd often cheered her up. "Chipmunk Rag" was simple and one of her earliest pieces. At first she tried the right hand, playing slowly to make sure of getting every note correct. Playing it over until it was natural under her fingers. She did the same for the left. Initially, when she put her hands together, her playing was faltering but soon, as her confidence grew, so did the speed. Playing was liberating. If she could make Imogen see her, she would have a life. The three of them could be happy. She wouldn't be able to leave the house at first but in time she might be able to control where she went. Maybe she'd be able to go on dinner dates with Simon. They could be a couple again, even lovers. For now, she'd focus on her life here. But in the future, she would find a way to see Simon too.

The piano lid slammed shut. Imogen collected up the music in her arms and locked the piano lid. Adelaide was shocked; she hadn't even heard Imogen enter the room. She followed as Imogen hurried away.

"Imogen, it's me, Ade." Imogen gave no indication she could hear her. But she had heard the piano. This was proof. Adelaide was elated; now she just had to get her to see and talk to her. Imogen was scared and would need coaxing and encouragement: it was an unusual situation for all of them. But now there was real hope.

"Did you write this?" Imogen held a note up at Jack's duvet-clad body. He was still asleep. Imogen shook his shoulder and he rolled, groaning as he emerged from sleep.

"What!?" Groggy, he sat up as she waved the piece of paper in his face. He grabbed it from her. It read, "I love you. Ade." She didn't allow him to answer.

"And this." She threw the picture of Imogen and Adelaide, which usually sat on top of the piano, in his lap. "Did you put this by the bed?"

Leaning against the windowsill, Adelaide was watching. She wondered why Imogen would think Jack had put them there.

"As a joke. Did you do it as a joke?" Adelaide thought it wouldn't have been a particularly funny joke.

"Why on earth would I do that? It wouldn't be a very funny joke." Adelaide nodded in agreement.

"I don't know." Covering her face, Imogen cried. "But what the hell were they doing there?"

"Sweetie, calm down. Maybe Nell put the photo

there because she knows how much you miss Ade."
He put his arms around her but she wriggled free.

"What about the note? Did she write that?"
Screwing up the note, she threw it on the floor.

"No, I guess not. It's probably an old one she
found in a drawer," he offered. Imogen was silent
for a moment, thinking.

"Do you think Nell remembers Ade very well?"

"I guess so, it hasn't been that long and they
were close. Why?"

"She's been saying and doing some weird things
lately. Talking about a lady reading her a story, and
she spelled 'Ade' with her bricks. I've just tried to
move on and keep things normal, so the kids don't
grow up in a sad house. Maybe I should talk about
Ade more, but I can't. It's too hard."

"I don't think you should make a big deal of
it. If she does anything else, ignore it. She'll soon
forget. Kids do."

This wasn't what Adelaide had expected.
Imogen didn't need to live in a sad house cleansed
of her memory. Adelaide would have to make her
understand they could be happy together again.

As teenagers, hiding one of her sister's shoes was one
of the tactics Adelaide had employed if she didn't
want Imogen to come out with her, and one Imogen
had used when she didn't want Adelaide to go out

without her. With only two years difference between their ages, their social circles had overlapped. Or more exactly, Imogen had infiltrated Adelaide's. Their parents joked that Imogen had become her shadow. At first, the disappearing shoes had been a prank both girls found funny.

Imogen was sure to understand what a missing shoe would mean. But taking away one boot of her favourite pair hadn't even been noticed. After looking for a few minutes, slightly late and a bit annoyed, she'd just worn an alternative pair. Using a black plastic sack, Adelaide took one shoe from every pair that Imogen owned and put it in the bag. She even took the posh, "going out" ones. She'd done this before. On the evening of her school leaving celebrations, Imogen, as usual, had insisted she'd come along. Adelaide didn't usually mind, but she'd wanted this occasion to be sister-free; an event special to her and her friends. Secretly, Adelaide was jealous. Imogen smoked and hung around at break times with the cool smoking gang, who congregated at the bottom of the sports field. Hilarious when drunk, Imogen drank all the more for entertainment value. She even had more experience with boys than Adelaide. Adelaide had been cast as the boring, responsible older sister, trying to keep Imogen out of trouble. Imogen was more fun and definitely less uptight. The night of the sixth-form party, Adelaide wanted to let go of her prim sensibilities and have a great night out. To make sure Imogen couldn't come along, Adelaide had collected one shoe of every pair she owned and hidden them in the loft. Imogen was furious and sulked for over a week.

Now though, Imogen was hysterical. She tore open every cupboard searching for her shoes. Jack and Elinor watched as she marched around ransacking the house. The contents of every cupboard were strewn across the floor.

"You did this!" she screamed at Jack as yet more rubbish was ejected from its storage space.

"Why would I? Imogen, this is madness."

"I'll bet it was you." She turned on Elinor, shouting. "Get my shoes now!"

Elinor began to cry. Imogen was out of control. Adelaide had been sure Imogen would understand and laugh. To blame Elinor was ridiculous. Pushing the bag from the top of the stairs, Adelaide watched from the landing as it flopped down over each step. Imogen, Jack and Nell gathered around it. Jack shook his head at Imogen.

"I thought we'd agreed to underplay this. I'm taking Nell out for an ice-cream and giving you a chance to tidy up."

It was becoming obvious to Adelaide that Imogen was closed to her. Wilfully obtuse, she suspected. Rejected and frustrated, the new life she'd dreamed of was slipping away. Imogen was a coward: she didn't want to find out if a new life was even possible for them.

Adelaide wouldn't be ignored.

It was Adelaide's turn to be Imogen's shadow. When Imogen tidied up, Adelaide followed – untidying. As Imogen replaced Elinor's books and toys, Adelaide rearranged them. If the oven was on low, she turned it up to its highest setting. At night, she'd rearrange items of furniture to suit her own preference. Carefully removing the contents of the airing cupboard, she laid them out in the hallway. The house keys were removed from Imogen's bag and placed in her coat pocket, and the car keys removed from their hook and left in a bowl in the dining room. But Imogen could have been a robot. She continued going about the daily duties she had been programmed to perform, ignoring the damage caused and starting over again.

Slowly but surely, with every correction the robot made, Adelaide became enraged.

Archie's tiny hands were clenched into fists and his arms were extended above his head. He was at peace. As Adelaide watched him sleep, she envied his lack of self-awareness; his body rose and fell with each breath. Regular in his feeding routine, Adelaide knew he'd wake up soon. Imogen was hugging Jack from behind and, sleeping side by side, they looked like the perfect adoring couple. Adelaide wondered how long Jack would remain oblivious to her struggle with Imogen. Wriggling in his cot, Archie began to wake up. A feeble squeak turned into a loud cry. Imogen opened her eyes and lay motionless for a moment. Crying, without even taking a breath, Archie's arms and legs were taut and still, suspended by his fury.

"Okay, sweetheart, Mummy's coming." Imogen sat up and swung her legs onto the floor. Again, she sat for a minute, rubbing her eyes. Adelaide stood observing her from just a few feet away. As Imogen walked to the cot, Adelaide stepped back to let her pass. Imogen lifted Archie from the cot and turned back towards the bed. As she did, Adelaide extended her foot. Imogen fell forward. Hard. And as she went down, her head clipped the edge of the bedside cabinet. Archie screamed as he hit the floor. Clamping her hand to her mouth, Adelaide recoiled with shock. She hadn't meant for Imogen or the baby to get hurt.

But then, as Adelaide thought about it, maybe this was what was needed to get her attention.

"We're all going on a summer holiday, no more

working for a week or two." Imogen was singing at Elinor who was struggling to pull a rucksack onto her back. She had a pair of sunglasses perched on her head.

"Holiday, hooray!" Elinor clapped. "Mummy, how long?"

"Daddy is just packing the car and then we'll be off."

"Hooray!" Elinor spun around. Adelaide was sitting at the dining room table watching the hustle of the holiday preparations. Imogen was taking Elinor away. Adelaide was being punished.

"Okay, that's the boot done. Anything else, Imogen?"

"Just the kids. Thanks for this, Jack." She kissed him on the cheek.

"If my lady needs a holiday, then that's what she shall have. I know it's been tough with Archie and Ade." Imogen turned away to see Elinor spinning round and round.

"Stop that, Nell, you'll be sick." Ignoring her mother, Elinor continued spinning. Archie was in his bouncy chair on the floor and she stumbled, landing on top of him.

"I told you to stop and now look what you've done." She dragged Elinor from the baby and held her by the arm. "Can you do nothing you're told?" Her spittle sprayed on Elinor's face. Adelaide was on her feet, ready to rescue the child, but Jack stepped in.

"Off to the toilet, you." He gently ushered her to the door. Archie was screaming. Imogen lifted him out of his chair and held him to her shoulder.

"It's okay, you're okay," she repeated as she paced the room. Adelaide watched Imogen with Archie; she looked content with him, but with Elinor she was short-tempered and resentful. It was wrong for Imogen to treat her children in such different ways. Imogen was not the mother Adelaide had thought she would be. Or the mother that Adelaide herself would have been. If the option hadn't been stolen from her.

"We're all going on a summer holiday." Jack was singing as he danced into the room with Elinor in his arms. "Come on, let's get going."

"I'll just get the baby's things. You get Elinor sorted."

"Aye, Aye, capt'n." Jack swept Elinor out of the door. Imogen laid the baby in his chair and checked through his bag. She added a packet of wipes, picked up the baby and left the house. Adelaide had been abandoned. Again.

The first thing Adelaide did was to make a replica of the calendar. They would only be gone for ten days, but to cross off each day as it passed would remind her that her solitary confinement was temporary. She was alone but at least she could look forward to Elinor's return.

Imogen used to say that she loved Ade, that she couldn't bear to lose her. But now that they'd been given a chance to be together again she was ignoring her. It had been naive to think that Imogen had ever really cared about her. To think that Imogen was turning away made Adelaide sad, angry and confused. The certainties her security was built on were unravelling. Like finally admitting she was jealous of Imogen's social skills, she now conceded she'd tricked herself into believing they loved each other equally. It was obvious. Imogen had always been a selfish brat. She had only wanted Ade for her friends. Wearing Ade's brand new clothes and sneaking her coat over them before Adelaide could see, and then revealing them to her friends and getting all the credit. New lipsticks were mutilated and eye shadows gouged from their packaging. Their relationship was only good because Adelaide had invariably let Imogen have her own way.

And Imogen knew that Elinor had been a joy to her when she was dying. Her laughter had kept her sane. Now Imogen was keeping them apart. Adelaide was perplexed at how Imogen could be so cruel.

Sun shone through the windows making the interior of the house feel dark. Longing to go outside, in compensation she opened all the windows as far as they would stretch and stood in the middle of the living room holding out her arms, relishing the cool breeze that blew throughout the house. She would at least enjoy being in the living world where she could do almost whatever she liked.

Imogen was predictable. Adelaide opened the lid to her jewellery box and there was the key to the piano. The music had just been dumped on the ottoman. Each morning she crossed the day off her makeshift calendar and then played the piano. In the afternoon she read a new book. Imogen didn't have a very good collection and loved detective fiction. Adelaide wouldn't have read this kind of material, but now she devoured the stories of Sherlock Holmes and Hercule Poirot. At least it was new. Action films and reality TV shows, which she would have abhorred, she now enjoyed.

She was living again.

At night she slept in Elinor's bed. It made her feel close to her. The bed was a little too short, but she didn't mind curling up until she fitted in a snug ball. Keeping the night-light on, she read the titles of the books adorning the shelves. Adelaide imagined reading them with Elinor and practised the conversations they would have. They would of course point out the pictures and laugh at the jokes, but she could also help teach her to read. She'd just started school and Imogen was too busy with the baby. Adelaide could make Elinor's education a project. But there was no way she could enjoy the piano with Elinor unless Imogen accepted her.

Her anger at Imogen for taking Elinor away was flourishing. Memories from childhood popped into her head, triggered by everyday items. The carpet sweeper, which had become a family heirloom, reminded Adelaide how Imogen would do anything to get praise from their mother. Any opportunity to help out with housework was an opportunity to suck up. Their mother's request for someone to "put the carpet sweeper round" saw Imogen, within thirty seconds, dancing across the floor, pushing it back and forth in rhythmic action. On Sundays, Imogen would be up weighing ingredients in preparation for her baking session with their mother. At teatime, she'd parade into the living room, carrying a baked masterpiece oozing with fruit and cream. Their Dad would "ooh" and "ah". "Isn't she a clever clogs?" he'd say. And Ade agreed, being benevolent and good-natured; after all, cleaning and baking weren't her thing. But the truth was now obvious. Imogen had insisted on being the favourite, the only daughter who counted.

Reassessing the past led her to relive the painful split with her first boyfriend. Adelaide didn't want to think it but it was too late, the thought had already occurred. Tom was perfect as far as Adelaide was concerned. He possessed the trio of goodness: height, an athletic build and thick blonde hair, which he flicked back from his face to reveal deep-brown eyes. She was so in love.

When she'd walked in on Imogen and Tom kissing, her first thought was that he'd betrayed her. Imogen confirmed it.

"Honestly, Ade, I turned around and there he was. He didn't give me a chance to stop him." Adelaide believed her and ended the relationship. Heartbroken, Adelaide had cried every day for a term. Over the years, Imogen claimed she'd done her a favour and saved her more heartache; she'd also never have met Simon if it hadn't been for her. Adelaide had been a gullible idiot.

Each day that passed, bringing their return nearer, led Adelaide to fantasise about how she could force Imogen to acknowledge her. She'd give it one last attempt for them all to be together – it was only reasonable – but after that she'd have to find a different solution to be with Elinor.

When Elinor came through the front door, Adelaide wanted to rush to her and hug her but Imogen was directly behind, ushering her up the hallway.

"Come on, slowcoach. Archie needs a nappy change." Elinor saw Adelaide and ran towards her.

"Heeelloooo!" She held out a colourful wind-mill. "Look what I've got."

Imogen stopped and stared towards where Adelaide was standing. For a moment she thought Imogen could see her.

"Hello, Imogen. I'm still waiting here. For you. For Elinor. For us."

"We're not staying here." Imogen turned and left the house. Elinor remained where she was.

"And I'm not going anywhere!" Adelaide shouted to Imogen, who was strapping Archie back in the car.

"Come and get in the car, Elinor." Imogen was standing by the driver's door. "Leave that, Jack." Jack was unpacking the boot. Bemused, he slammed it shut.

"I'll count to five, Elinor."

"No. I won't come," Elinor shouted back. She stood in the doorway.

"One." Both Imogen and Elinor stood firm. "Two." Jack walked towards Imogen.

"Not again, as soon as we get home, this is ludicrous. Come inside and we can sort it out." Imogen turned on him.

"I don't expect you to understand. Three."

"You go and do what you need to do and I'll stay here with Nelly." He turned away and walked towards the house. Imogen got into the car and started the engine.

Elinor cried, "Mummy!" The child panicked and ran out towards the car as Imogen reversed into the road. Adelaide flung herself after her, yelling, "Wait! Nell!" and stepped out of the front door.

"Nell!" She was still running. Hector looked up from the sofa. Adelaide ran to the door and pulled on the handle. It remained closed. She shook it, crying with anger and kicking the door.

"Please open, please let me go back."

Hector was watching her with sleepy half interest. Death suited him. But then, it was a lot like his life. "What are you looking at?" Adelaide snarled at him and battled the urge to kick him across the room.

Accidents happen. And in less than a moment. Elinor might be hurt and there was no way Adelaide could find out. She was stuck in this house while her new life and Elinor were elsewhere. She couldn't keep her safe. Adelaide punched the wall in frustration. But then, it had been Imogen who put Elinor in harm's way. It was Imogen who was at fault: Imogen was an unfit mother.

The box hit the landing with force and dust

billowed into the air. Opening the lid, half a dozen faces stared up at her. All the soft toys she couldn't bear to throw away, but hadn't had room for when she'd left home, had been stowed in the loft. Her favourites were Walter, a large tortoise, and Sausage Legs Fatty, a pink-faced knitted doll with stumpy arms and legs. Arranging them on her brother's bed, she thought about how she could sleep with Elinor and sooth her when she woke in the night. Adelaide would be able to devote her time to Elinor. She'd tried to reconnect with Imogen, and she'd tried hard, but now she knew how futile it was. Imogen had never loved her and then she'd tried to take Elinor away, even though she knew that the child made her life worthwhile: Imogen was a monster.

But Adelaide had worked out the solution to her problem; she just had to wait for the front door to open.

"Look at the stars, Nell, they're beautiful." Elinor stood on the ledge of the open window. She looked up into the sky as Adelaide held her around the waist. Adelaide would have to push Elinor very hard to make sure she fell with enough force to die.

"Would you like to come and stay with Auntie Adelaide?" Elinor nodded. Adelaide kissed her on the cheek. "We'll have fun and I'll take good care of you."

The light flicked on.

"You're not taking her anywhere." Imogen was standing behind them and holding out her arms. "Come to Mummy, Nell." Her voice was calm, caring and in charge. Elinor shook her head and clung onto Adelaide's neck.

Adelaide was confused. "Imogen?"

"I've been able to see you for a while. Since you took my shoes."

"But then, why ..." The anger engulfed Adelaide. Imogen interrupted her.

"Because it isn't right. It isn't natural." She was as determined as Adelaide was enraged.

"We still have a chance of living together. What we've always planned. You, me and Elinor."

"It isn't living, Ade." Imogen took a step nearer.

"You don't want that? Well, I don't want you anyway. But I do want Nell." She started to peel Elinor's arms from her neck, ready to push her from the window. Imogen edged further forward.

"It's not fair, Ade, she deserves to live."

"She will be living. With me." Elinor was beginning to panic, confused by their words. She let go of Adelaide and dropped to the floor, turning towards Imogen. Catching hold of her hair, Adelaide yanked her back, securing her under her arm. Imogen continued with her implacable calmness.

"I'm so sorry you were young and you suffered,

but it doesn't mean you have the right to take my child."

Adelaide hoisted Elinor onto the windowsill. The child screamed and clung to the frame, pushing back as Adelaide tried to force her through it. Imogen ran the last few steps.

"Hold on, Nelly!" Pulling Adelaide with all her strength, Imogen yanked one arm free from the child. It put Adelaide off balance and she fell backwards, dragging the child with her. Elinor screamed again, "Mummy!", and held out her arms. Imogen grabbed her. The three grappled and clung together on the floor, entangled, all fighting a grim battle. Then, with a strength that was almost superhuman, Imogen severed herself and her daughter free.

Looking down at Adelaide on the floor, Imogen was crying, her calm broken.

"Adelaide, I've missed you every day, all the time. I loved you but your time is over, you have to leave us alone. We need a normal life."

*****

As usual, Hector was snuggled next to Adelaide on the sofa, snoozing. She flicked through the TV channels, searching for the least unbearable repeat. Death was so unendurably boring. And it had given her plenty of opportunity to repent of her life. It was her own fault if she hadn't made the most of things before her time ran out: it had been too easy to lead a half life. Her second chance hadn't worked out either.

A familiar breeze cooled her leg. She leaned forward to look; the front door was open. Adelaide got up, crossed the room and slammed the door shut before returning to the couch. The living world was no longer her concern. But Adelaide was sure there had to be something more. And she was ready for it. Fully and completely.

RE: MYSTERIOUS PAMPHLET: EXPERT OPINION

Dear Dr Phillips,

I hope you don't mind me contacting you. I read your book, *Hearth and Home: Understanding Pre-Christian Mythology of Northern Europe*, published last year.

Please find attached a scanned copy of a pamphlet I recently acquired. I think it might interest you. I'm hoping you will be able to offer your opinion as a world-renowned expert on paganism and folklore.

The pamphlet was written in 1897 by a Henry Scott, and as yet I've been unable to find any other record of him. His story is extraordinary and, although it would be easy to dismiss it as outlandish fiction, there is something in his tone which makes me feel uneasy.

I've been an avid collector of Victorian pamphlets and periodicals for a number of years and have never come across anything of its nature before.

Any information you can give I'd be most grateful for. I've reread the pamphlet at least a dozen times and can't help feeling increasingly intrigued.

Many thanks.

Yours,

Ms Joyce Fry
94 Eastgrove Drive
Hove
BN3 2AY
England

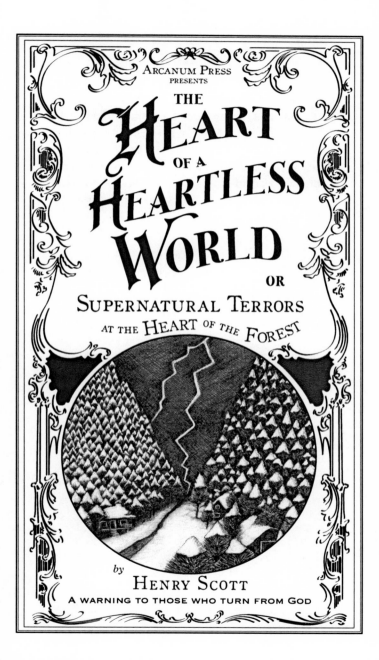

ARCANUM PRESS
PRESENTS

THE
HEART
OF A
HEARTLESS
WORLD

OR

SUPERNATURAL TERRORS
AT THE HEART OF THE FOREST

by

HENRY SCOTT

A WARNING TO THOSE WHO TURN FROM GOD

This pamphlet is a warning to the arrogant, the weak and the misguided. For those who believe Man alone can explain the natural world and live without God. Such naiveté! It is a grave mistake to treat nature as the plaything of humanity; nowhere is this more evident than in the forests of the North. For those who fail to respect the earth and her secrets, let this be a warning.

How proud, how arrogant I was. She looked into my heart and saw the hole I'd hidden there. My loneliness was laid bare to her and she pursued me to fill my void, not with a love, fair and true, but with horrors of lasciviousness and wanton passion. Mine was a Godless soul without Divine Grace. And she did soothe me, taking me far into the heart of her. Like the smoke from the opium pipe, I drifted deeper into her soul and further from my own.

If only I had heeded the warnings that the villagers gave in their looks and sighs, but my determination to seek out the native flora and fauna of the woods was such that none could deter me, nor even cast a shadow into my mind. The sum of my goals was to make my name in the Natural Sciences, and prove to my father and beloved Emily that my loss of faith was a rational choice, founded in my complete trust in science. With devoted conviction, I believed science would grant mankind truth and knowledge superior to the mythologies and falsehoods of religion. So equipped, we would build a superior civilization for our children. This was progress, as I perceived it; I intended to be a part of it.

My plan entailed undertaking the journey made by my hero, the Swedish

botanist and physician, Carl Linnaeus. By way of a private auction, I had acquired a notebook Linnaeus had made whilst writing his masterpiece, *Flora Lapponica.* Throughout, there were vexing clues and references to unexplained encounters—encounters with the natural world, which civilization was not yet ready to accept. Given the reception Mr. Darwin's theory had been given, I was not surprised Linnaeus would need to withhold the controversial, writing as he was in the 1730s. I wanted to be sure: make records of any botanical and zoological discoveries, and take photographs of any such forest life. For posterity's sake, I was to keep a personal journal detailing my findings. Thank God for the mysterious root pushed into my hand by an old man of the village: my first discovery. Initially, I thought it to be some drug taken by the locals to endure the boredom of the long, dark winter nights. It caused me some distress to think of the powers of seduction

it held; I was to discover it would save my life.

I had just turned twenty-eight when I set out on my adventure. It was the 14th of March of the year of our Lord 1896 and I was high in spirit, with much hope for my future. Without success, I could not hope to win back the esteem of my father or the hand of my childhood sweetheart, Emily. The journey to Uppsala University was to take a full two weeks and although challenging—I am not a seafarer by any definition—it would not be as arduous as my previous sea voyages across the Indian Ocean. Taking the train from London, I travelled north to Hull; from there I took the steamer to Hamburg. Where my onward journey was not possible, I rested overnight. The passage from Hamburg to Gothenburg was rough, making me so ill as the vessel lurched and tipped that I was confined to my cabin for the entire crossing. My heart was filled with relief and terror as we came in sight of the

Bohuslän coast.

A thunderous storm raged, and thick, churning snow obscured my vision until forked lightening ruptured the sky, illuminating the brooding landscape. Small, red, wooden houses nestled amongst the snow-heavy evergreens, taking refuge from the tempest. Entirely surrounding the simple dwellings, trees contorted, bending over the roofs, giving the impression of both guardians and keepers.

Gothenburg was a lively and bustling city with a population of around 100,000, although, after the crowds of London, it had the feel of a self-important town. Being Sweden's major port, it was affluent and grand, dominated by mighty merchants' houses and an impressive City Hall. From high in its tower, the clock kept watch over the town square, and I reflected that I would soon be far removed from human life and the clockwork machinery of industrialization. I took full advantage

of the comforts of the Hotel Haglund, and was grateful for its opulence after the hardship of my sea-crossing. This would be the last luxury I would encounter before my journey into the wilderness. On unpacking, I discovered that an essential part to my camera had been damaged on my stormy voyage. I was obliged to wait at Gothenburg for two nights further, until the replacement part arrived.

When finally I boarded the night train to Stockholm, I had so much joy for my blessed future: a future of my own design and making. But that night, a cloud marred the enjoyment of my reflections. I dreamt I was trapped in a long, slender train corridor, running on and on, jolting against the sides, and as the panic rose in my throat, the passage would suddenly turn into another, more enclosed and claustrophobic than the last. Strips of light pinewood covered the walls, floor and ceiling, and the only details apparent on these surfaces were the knots found at the heart of a tree. Beautiful singing filled the compartment, which smelt like freshly sawn wood. Instead of lighting my spirit, the sound filled me with dread as I fled down the corridors trying to escape its dominating allure. I awoke, perspiring and confused, the gentle rocking motion of the moving train drawing me slowly back to my senses. Looking out of the window onto the light-blue dawn, I saw the flat still surface of a lake chopped into segments by the regimented evergreens, still heavy with the last snow of winter. Watching for a moment, shards of golden sunlight sliced past the tree trunks to warm my face. The next sound I heard was a shrill train whistle, alerting passengers we were soon to arrive at Stockholm.

Due to my delay at Gothenburg, I was keen to make my connection north to Uppsala. After a satisfying breakfast, I joined the train that would take me onward. Snow-drenched trees, frozen lakes and vast tracts of open land passed by as I reviewed my arrangements and commitments for the coming week. Upon arrival, I was met by Professor Rydberg, the head of the botany department, who I confess was much younger than I had expected, considering his position and reputation. His deep-green eyes peered from between a long fringe and a thick beard.

"I wanted to greet you in person and get an impression of the man who is to teach us of Linnaeus's work." He laughed as he said this and held out his hand. I was embarrassed.

"No, I admire ..." Cutting me off, he laughed again, slapped me on the back and pushed me up into the cart. For the rest of the journey he hummed to himself, occasionally pointing out places of local interest.

I was to stay for six nights, meet with staff of both the botany and zoology departments, and give a lecture on my thesis and reasons for the journey. This was whilst all the time gathering my equipment and supplies for

my investigation.

My student rooms were basic but comfortable and I prepared for my lecture with great anticipation. Embarrassed by Professor Rydberg's comments, I revisited my own notes and Linnaeus's *Flora Lapponica* to ensure I would not misinterpret the master's work in front of his own countrymen and scientific descendants. I wanted to be clear of my own assertion of its intentional omissions, but didn't intend to make a full confession of what I'd read in the notebook for fear of ridicule. Proof would be required for that. The thought of making myself a fool in front of such esteemed gentlemen filled me with horror.

The lecture was met with a combination of curiosity, admiration and good humour. On the suggestion that Linnaeus had omitted particular species civilization had yet to prepare for, there was much mirth. Some students joked that one should look to the folklore of the villages to solve such mysteries.

"Be careful, Mr. Scott, so deep in the forest, you may be spirited away." They mocked and I laughed along. We agreed that science had surely usurped the human need for superstition and tales of faerie folk.

As did Linnaeus, I intended to travel on foot and by horse. I had learnt to ride and hunt in the army; jungle was familiar terrain and I expected to encounter similar issues in the dense forests. The horse selected for my journey was a fine beast. He answered to the name of Sotis, being black as soot. Using Linnaeus's original map was crucial in keeping with his route. I also packed a sextant and compass. A sextant would be useless in the canopied forest interior but helpful along the coast. Once I turned inland, I would make a detailed log of my bearing and distances. One could not be too careful. Linnaeus had travelled clockwise around the coast of the Gulf of Bothnia, making major inland incursions from Umeå, Luleå and Tornio. I differed in that I had given myself seven months, instead of Linnaeus's six, wanting to get used to the terrain and take a little time to savour the 1,200 mile expedition. I was due to return in October, having gathered information, made sketches and taken photographs of the mysterious unnamed omissions from Linnaeus's *Flora Lapponica*. My curiosity extended to customs of the native Sami people, the reindeer-herding nomads who wander Scandinavia's vast tundras, as well as the lives of the hunters and woodmen who frequented the forests.

Sotis and I prospered as we made our way north, stopping to inspect the flora and fauna we came across and cross-referencing it in the *Flora Lapponica*. We rose with the sun and, as the sun withdrew, made sure to have the camp set up and the fire built before the temperature dropped. For the first few weeks, I had ample provisions, but after that I was to hunt for meat and gather berries. Of course, having been in the army, none of this was unbeknownst to me—but how different the cold forests of the North were to the dusty heat of India.

The forests struck me with awe and wonder. They are vast, and in certain places so dense that there was the constant impression of dusk. Only by looking up to the sky could any daylight be discerned. At night, it is so dark that one cannot see more than a few feet in front of one's face. I kept my rifle with me at all times and listened carefully for the approach of hungry wolves and bears. Sometimes, the cries of wolves could be heard howling far off and it soothed me to know they were at a distance. It is a curious thing that even though I am a man of science and have a perfect understanding of the natural world, away from the lights of civilization the atmosphere of the woods put me in mind of trolls, sprites and other supernatural creatures. One clear evening, I was fortunate enough to see pink–green fingers mutating and stretching far across the sky. The streams of light moved in and out of one another, intertwining, meeting and then releasing. The contrast of these glorious Aurora Borealis with the pitch black forest made it possible for me to imagine a time before rationality, before Man understood The Law of Natural Selection. How reasonable it would have been to invent supernatural stories to explain the terror of the wilderness.

On my journey I passed through many hamlets. It was bewildering to observe the look of true horror and fear on the faces of the villagers as I told them of my intentions. I felt it sad that they were unable to embrace our contemporary understanding of nature. I was sure that there was nothing that a fire, warm coat and a rational mind could not solve.

After a few weeks, I reached the village that was to be my last contact with humanity for a long stretch. There, an old man of the village had, with profound desperation, pushed a root into my palm. Naturally, I attempted to ask him what it was and about its purpose, but he shook his head, refusing to take it back, unwilling to listen to my enquiries. The *Flora Lapponica* had no corresponding entry. This was very pleasing as it was my first new discovery, and I had the honour of recording and naming it. What the old man imagined I was to do with the root I did not know. I transferred it to my bag and thought no more of it. I left Sotis in the care of the village stables and set off into the woods.

Six weeks into my journey, the weather improved greatly, the nights never getting darker than a shadowy blue dusk, even at the midnight hour. When I happened upon a clearing, it was a joy to feel the sun upon my face and see the blue sky above giving relief from the murky twilight of the forest. By this time, I was getting used to life in the wilderness, and although I

was not an expert in hunting for the small animals that had become my main diet, it was becoming a little easier. There was sometimes a gap of days between catches, but I managed to eat well. I confess that, at this time, I was beginning to feel a little alone and started to talk aloud to myself to break the monotony of the forest silence. Whilst sleeping, I sometimes dreamt of the beautiful but dreadful song I had heard on my train journey and would wake to the grateful relief of silence.

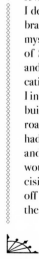

It was Midsummer's eve, and I decided to join in the celebrations by making a feast for myself. "Midsummer" is one of Sweden's main festivals and demonstrates their dedication to the pagan calendar. I intended to hunt for elk and built a large fire on which to roast it. By this time, I only had a little ammunition left and knew that my success would depend on the precision of my shooting. I set off into the wood, tracking the pathways that had been

worn into the forests by elk and hunter. After walking for a short while, I heard movement amongst the trees ahead and stopped to listen. I stayed still for some time, ears straining, but only silence returned so, content, I continued heading in the same direction. It was then that a small light became discernible through the trees, some three hundred feet in front of me. My curiosity much aroused, I followed, imagining that it must be the light of a woodsman or hunter. Considering my increasing need to converse with another person, I moved quickly through the woods towards it. As I grew closer, the light seemed to recede into the forest and, as an increasing compulsion made me follow, I pushed further through the trees, never minding where I trod or the density of the bracken I waded through. The light moved steadily, its power growing with intensity. The brighter the light, the calmer I felt, as if I were a babe resting at the bosom of my mother. The trees started to withdraw their branches and the bracken withered, allowing me to pass. The forest bowed down to me, soothing and kind, as if it would not let a creature cause me harm. The only sound was the beating of my heart in rhythm with the trees, birds and beasts of the forest. The light glowed brighter and brighter until it illuminated the forest, which shone under its protection. Peace filled my heart and I cared for naught but to stay under the safety of the light.

Then it stopped.

I was lost. Checking my watch, compass and map, I found I had wandered over three miles from my camp and it was only a few moments later than when I had set out on my hunt. I could not for the life of me understand how I had covered so much ground in so short a time and without being aware of how I had done so. It was as if the time had been stolen. But the white forest light had embued such a feeling of peace that I was not the

least downhearted at having to find my way back.

As the imprint of the forest light began to fade, I once again longed for human company. I spent many hours recreating in my mind the moment I would be deemed a great success, standing on the podium in front of an esteemed audience, all there to hear of the discoveries I alone had made. Emily would laugh and clap at my triumph and she would come back to me, smiling, loving and gentle, as I had known her as a child.

My nightmares increased, and the singing haunted my sleeping hours. The voice was trying to lure me into the deepest woods, a part of the forest unknown and forbidden to mankind, where, once entered, there would be no hope of escape. But that was of little importance, for it was a safe place, where one would no longer know pain or loneliness, only comfort and peace. I could not distinguish the words of the song but its meaning was clear, carried with every note

A strange light in the forest

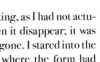

being observed. The memory of the dream lingered in my bones, causing me to face the stark reality that there was nowhere I could find solace: the love I had experienced from my mother as a child was the only unconditional love I have ever felt. But she was long since gone. Even Emily had broken our engagement when I, as she perceived it, turned away from God.

The sensation of being watched dogged me until I became frantic. North, south, east and west; I felt exposed on all sides, there being no protection wherever I moved. Then I discerned in the distance, slightly obscured by the trees, the outline of a figure, almost a blue shadow, a twilight reflection. The figure was slender and the line of the head fine, it stood precise and still amongst the woods. I stared for a moment, arrested, until the call of a wolf broke my fixed state and I ran forward, calling out to it. But as I moved, the figure was no longer there. It

was vexing, as I had not actually seen it disappear; it was simply gone. I stared into the woods where the form had been. I have no memory of how long I stood there, but it was dusk when I once again came to my senses.

After these strange incidents, I reflected on the words of the laughing Uppsala students and their jovial concern I might be spirited away by supernatural creatures. For a moment I wished to be safe, back in company and the luxury of the Hotel Haglund.

From this time on, I experienced a constant feeling of dread, as if I were an animal being stalked. Throwing myself into my research, I increased the pace of my travels, forcing my way through the forest. I no longer enjoyed my work and was quick at analysing the samples, taking little time to study the specimens in great detail. I longed to leave the claustrophobic enclosure of the forest and to return to the village to be reunited

with Sotis, but it was at least a week's journey and the coast another three. I decided to make haste and leave as soon as I felt I had analysed enough samples from this particular area. Having made this decision, I felt lighter of heart and returned to my work with purpose. As I journeyed through the forest, I was happy at the idea of human contact, but I often had to stop and rest from moments of exhaustion. Since the onset of my disturbing dreams, my sleep had become irregular and erratic. I would wake in the middle of the day with a plant sample in my hand, where I had succumbed to sleep without notice. Due to exhaustion, it became harder to ensnare the small animals that had become the staple of my diet, and I went longer between meals. By this point, I had only a half dozen shells for my rifle and I was determined to keep these as protection from wolves and bears. Although I feared that if I did not allow myself to use the rifle to catch food, I

would soon be too weary to continue the journey onward and escape the forest.

On one of my successful attempts at ensnaring a creature, so happy was I at seeing a rabbit in the trap, I fumbled with fatigue and joy as the creature struggled. I lost grip and it escaped, darting from my fist into the undergrowth. I collapsed onto the ground, hopeless and defeated, placing my head into my hands.

"You should try using a bow and arrow."

So stunned was I by the violent intrusion of the human voice that I scrambled back into the bracken. However, there was something calming and reassuring in its tone and pitch; I was relieved by the mix of command, sympathy and clarity.

"I'm sorry, I have shocked you." There was faint amusement in her voice. I looked ahead to see the bottom of her dress and slowly raised my eyes. It was a moment before I could make sense of what I saw before me. Surrounded by a very slight light, she almost

imperceptibly vibrated, like heat from a desert mirage. She was gold, red, orange and green; all the colours of nature at once. Her hair flowed, and seemed to balance her, functioning as the tail of an animal would. For the briefest of moments, as she smiled, I saw Emily smiling down at me with loving kindness and my heart leapt up to her. My emotions warred within me, making me long to be in Emily's embrace, whilst simultaneously I wanted to be nowhere else but here with this beautiful creature. She held up an elegant set of bow and arrows. They reflected gold in the barest of light.

"I will teach you."

She offered her slender hand and with an unnatural strength pulled me to my feet.

"You will never be hungry in the forest again."

I could not speak, but just stared as she lifted the bow to her shoulder, pulled back the string and released the arrow into the forest. I heard the impact and something fall

through the branches. On the ground at my feet lay a dead bird. I gazed at the bird and then at the woman who had delivered it. There was something animalistic about her, as she seemed to constantly listen to the forest, but she never took her eyes from me. Second to second, she merged and emerged, blending into the trees whilst always being perfectly present. She smiled, awaiting approval; her red hair was sleek and reminiscent of the fox, her body slender and her movements elegant, quick, and economical. She held out the bow and indicated for me to take it.

"You try." She nodded her encouragement.

I took it and looked at her, perplexed and embarrassed. She nodded again, so I raised the bow to my shoulder and loaded the arrow. It slotted into position with ease. I drew it back and an energy surged through my body; I felt powerful and strong, embodying all the energy of the forest. Releasing the arrow, I once again heard the

sound of a deadweight falling through the trees. A bird lay in my hand. Exhilarated and terrified, I threw it and the bow to the ground. Turning to the woman, I sought approval and reassurance, as a young child from its mother. She was gone.

Hunger triumphed over fear; I immediately built a fire and prepared a meal of the two birds. My exhilaration continued and the feeling I'd had a spectacular but terrifying dream lingered. Daring not to touch the bow that lay on the ground but a few feet away, I often looked over to it as physical proof of what had happened. Now, satiated from my meal, the fear began to subside. The relief that I would not die alone in the forest replaced my concerns and I soon fell asleep.

Pulling Emily's hair at the back of her neck, I forced her into a deep kiss; she struggled, I persisted, pushing my tongue into her mouth, forcing it wider, and clasping her tightly, close into my body, thrusting my

aroused member into her sex. She struggled harder, but the more she tried to withdraw, the stronger my grasp. We were being watched. The forest woman stood by laughing and nodding, encouraging me to continue. To please her, I complied. Horrified, I realized Emily was sobbing, hurting under my hold, but I could not stop, so eager was I to please the forest woman. As her laughter increased, I grasped harder and harder. Emily fought and begged, but I would not stop. I jolted up straight, shocked awake through fear—fear of what I had been capable of and fear of the cruelty below the surface of my cultured veneer.

Emily had warned that if I rejected God I'd be vulnerable to temptation and sin. I'd laughed, confident at my own strength of will: this had shaken my certainty. The forest was calm; the trees were still and sure, upright, standing to attention. My fire was out and I looked to where the bow had been. Instead of where I had left

First contact with the Forest Woman

it at the far side of the fire, it was neatly laid in front of me. Scrambling to my feet I ran into the forest, searching, desperate, for what at that time I could not tell.

I continued my work, fully intending to carry out my plan to leave the forest, but I became increasingly fearful that I would never see the woodland woman again. Struggling with my loneliness and the respite she had bestowed, gave me much confusion. I was unable to account for her presence in the forest and her mysterious gift. Vexed at her strange appearance, both solid as the trees and as changeable as the light, I delighted in her restful smile and reassuring voice. But a creeping terror pulsed in my veins as I remembered my nightmare. Her encouraging smile a fixed image in my head, with ease she had watched as I subjected my darling Emily to such base and brutish behaviour. I had rejected the Christianity of my youth when I had decided on a

life of science. The works of Mr. Darwin had indeed convinced me that Divine Creation was to be rejected by the truly thinking man and that Marx was indeed right when he had asserted that, "Religion is the sign of the oppressed creature, the heart of a heartless world, just as it is the spirit of the spiritless situation." But my position in the wood was that of the "oppressed creature".

It was to the prayer book that my beloved Emily had given to me when I left for India, that I turned to ease my conflicted mind. The small volume had been in my breast pocket at all times since. Although I had protested at the time that it was not a gift I could appreciate, Emily was sure it would give me comfort when I was far from home. How wise and pure she is. Oh, Emily! If I had known then what I was to learn, I would have given up science to live a good and righteous life at your side.

It was of stories I'd heard as a child that my mind turned, tales of myths and

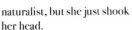

legends that tell of temptations from ungodly creatures, trying to pervert the good man from his spiritual Grace. To counter my fears, I read aloud from the prayer book, directing my words into the forest, attempting to protect myself from whatever dwelt there. I worked hard and sang, "Dear Lord and Father of Mankind" with as much gusto as I could muster. The louder I sang, the quicker I worked, bolstering my fortitude against temptation. But in my heart, I knew that I was already corrupted; my nightmare had shown me of what I truly fantasized.

My singing at least helped me to keep working and brought vivid memories of happy times I had spent with Emily. We had walked in the woods near to our childhood homes and I had told her the Latin names of the plants and trees. She had laughed:

"That's all very clever, Henry, but how will it keep us when we are married?"

I had told her that I would one day be a famous naturalist, but she just shook her head.

"Not if your father has anything to do with it. And I must say, darling, he may be right."

I'd tried to take this with good humour, but I knew that without my father's approval continuing with my studies would be impossible. The military career I had pursued to please him had left me dissatisfied and had become unendurable. I sang louder, trying to drown out the memory that had led to the source of my heartache. Gradually I noticed another melody begin to vibrate very quietly, almost inaudibly, coming in waves, carried on the breeze. I could not tell the direction from whence it came—it seemed to come from everywhere; each leaf, branch and plant emitted a vibration. It surrounded me, increasing in volume, mingling with my own song, raising my voice and enhancing its quality: I was, for the first time in my life, singing clear, tuneful tones. Never before had I sounded so sure of voice, but instead of "Dear Lord and Father of Mankind", I was now singing the song of my nightmare. But it was beautiful and good. I relished the alien words upon my tongue and, as they projected from my body, they became one with the vibrations of the forest; the trees began to glow and shine, approving of our mutual voice. I felt protected and safe, but exhilarated and powerful as I had when I drew back the bow the forest woman had bestowed upon me. The hole in my heart was mended and, at last, the ache I'd felt for so many years from the loss of my dear mother disappeared.

This was a revelation to me, and I at once felt at home in the forest. It was the first home I'd had since my mother's death. I made use of the bow and arrow and, to my amazement, with every arrow shot, an animal or bird was delivered. I laughed with relief and joy as I roasted the succulent meat. That evening, my sleep was deep and dreamless. In the morning,

I worked with relish. The thought of leaving the woods had been pushed from my mind. I journeyed deeper into the forest, singing the hymns I had learnt as a child, no longer afraid. It was then that my persistence was rewarded. As I stopped to inspect some plants, I came upon more and more varieties as yet uncategorized. How excited I was to photo-graph the specimens and record them in my journal. My mind again wandered to the time my work would be published to rapturous reception in London and beyond.

"You like the plants? They're good?"

I laughed with surprise and at her turn of phrase, which possessed a fond simplicity, as if I was a child and she had given me a treat, explaining that plants were my area of research and I was giving them names. She looked at me and frowned a little.

"The names Men give plants."

I was a little confused.

"I expect you're a committed Suffragette. Women in science are unnatural. They serve the species best when they continue it."

She smiled. "The forest is full of many things that Men do not understand, with your complicated explanations."

We both laughed.

"What does the box do?" She pointed to my camera.

I was taken aback, but I imagined that being so far north she had not yet come into contact with the modern technology. I explained that by using light, the box was able to take an impression of whatever I pointed to. I would then make a paper print of it. She frowned again.

"If you pointed it at me, you could take an impression of me?"

"Exactly. A picture-perfect impression."

She held out her hand for me to give it to her. I was pleased she was so interested. As I passed it over, the camera fell to the ground. I was stunned: it was as if she had willfully missed it, but

she immediately bent to retrieve it.

"Sorry. It is broken."

I stared at her.

"I'll take it with me and mend it. I'll bring it back anew."

"How will you do that? You didn't know what it was until a few moments ago."

"I'm good at making things. I made the bow and arrows."

She nodded, smiling. As I looked at the beautiful curve of her mouth my engineering knowledge receded to a part of my mind I couldn't access. My concerns dissolved and I allowed her to take it. She walked into the forest smiling and waving, holding up her small, delicate hand. When I looked back, she had disappeared. Soon after she had gone, I fell asleep. On waking a good few hours later, once again my energy had revived. Pleased I no longer experienced the terrible nightmares that had become a regular feature of sleep, I held an excitement as a small child returning home to his mother after an

endless term at boarding school, so eager was I at seeing the woodland woman again. Although I didn't wholly realize it at that time, I would have sacrificed any number of cameras to know that she would return to me once more. My loneliness abated with the knowledge of my forest friend.

After this, the woman came to see me every day. I journeyed, worked and sang, knowing that wherever I made my camp she would follow. Perplexed as I was at how she knew my whereabouts, I felt sure she would come. It was an unspoken arrangement and I never asked her what she did when we were apart. On her arrival, she would always ask the same eager question:

"You like the plants?"

To which I would answer, "How could I not?"

This went on until one day I said: "Do you know, I considered giving up and leaving the forest, thinking there was nothing to be found. I was also lonely, afraid."

She laughed and clapped her hands.

"And now you are happy because you are no longer lonely and there are many plants to be discovered."

She would often arrive without my being aware of her and would catch me singing at the top of my voice, enjoying the energy it embued me with, and the freedom it afforded.

Drop Thy still dews of quietness
Till all our strivings cease

"You no longer strive."
I jumped.

"No, the forest has been good to me, it will make my name."

"The forest is good to those who are good for it." She laughed.

"It's all been working out jolly well, at last. And I've found singing a comfort since I've been here. It stirs me on." I continued to sing.

Take from our souls the strain and stress
And let our ordered lives confess
The beauty of Thy peace.

On completing the lines, as before, a low vibration emitted from the forest around me, the sound increasing in volume, beautiful and seductive, lifting me out of myself and joining me as one with nature. Then she began to sing, the song of my dreams. As I opened my mouth to continue it was no longer "Dear Lord and Father of Mankind" that came from my lips, but her song once more. I could not understand or define the words that came out, only their meaning: I was safe and secure in the forest, welcomed by the creatures, plants and trees, none would harm me whilst I sang her song. The forest shone and glowed, its vibrations an accompaniment to our singing. As I watched her moving her small hand out to the forest, as if conducting it, I had no past and no future; there was only the present in the forest with her. My past fears and future ambitions, forgotten.

She drew me up into her eyes and pressed her lips against mine. As we embraced, her body enfolded me with such a passion I had never imagined possible. It brought me back to the nightmare of my wanton behaviour towards Emily. This time, however, it was the woman of the forest who was the target of my lust, and Emily watching in horror, angry and berating me for my base behaviour, but at the same time enjoying her triumphant vindication.

"I knew this is what you'd come to, brought so low by lust and moral weakness." Her tone was cruel and bitter, but shrill with excitement.

I fought with the woman, my hands pushing her away but my mouth desperate to continue tasting her. She was so strong, but didn't struggle or fight. She merely stepped away from me.

"You love someone else."

This was a statement, not a question. She stared at me, defiant as a child that has been denied sweets for bad behaviour. Her pride was hurt.

"I'm not the sort of chap

to go off with just any ..."

I stopped. But my meaning was true. Although science had taught me that it was natural to lie with a willing woman, the thought of Emily had stopped me. She was of the highest moral standing; we had never shared more than a tender kiss on the cheek, and I had not contemplated such a liaison with anyone, lest of all a woman who had thrown herself upon me. She cocked her head and shrugged.

"We shall see."

After this, I was afraid my woodland friend would not come again. I continued to find new, exotic plants and wildlife, and was reluctant to leave the forest as my work was progressing. Nonetheless, I was equally desperate to continue to feel the woodland peace and calm. I could no longer sing. My words had been stolen from me when she had turned away. Desperate to hear the forest vibrations, I listened, but none came. Silence endured. A fear crept over me that I was once again alone and I longed for the brief weeks of peace and safety I had encountered. My soul ached for comfort; my limbs were heavy with grief and my nightmares returned.

I was awoken with a gentle kiss upon my lips and as I opened my eyes it was into Emily's that I looked. With relief and pleasure, I returned her caress. We kissed with deepening passion and I felt released and free, realizing I'd been waiting to hold and be held by Emily for so very long. The kiss changed to something less tender but more vital, everything around me breathed a new life, the passion surged through my blood and every part of my body was awakened with new life. The forest was once again my home. I opened my eyes again to see the woodland woman staring back into mine. For a brief moment, I struggled against her, realizing that what I had taken for a dream was real, but she held me with such tender passions and soothing strokes that I

submitted under her touch.

From that moment on, I gave no thought to Emily and I longed only for the time when my woodland lady was by my side. Overwhelmed with joy and love for her and our woodland home, I worked, categorizing the numerous and varied new plants I found and sketched with such haste that I could barely hold the pencil. Without her, my mind wandered to the time she would be with me, and all the while she was with me I feared the moment she would leave. My work began to suffer, and although I had discovered more new varieties than I could ever have dreamt of, I soon found my mind had no thought other than of her. Trying to rest, I would often light a fire and lie beside it, hoping the warmth of the flame and its hypnotic dance would soon lead me to sleep. But as my eyes dropped closed, I would fall backwards into a dark abyss, never knowing how far I would fall or for how long. I would start awake in a panic, alone. It seemed that the time

between her visits became longer and I, helpless, had no idea where or how to find her. I became manic, pacing the forest, shouting into the trees for her to come. At the sight of her, all my anxiety would fade, forgotten, and when she kissed me, I felt the peace and safety she had bestowed on me when I first encountered her benevolence.

I lost all sense of time. The days began to draw in and the temperature dropped. I hardly gave any attendance to my worn appearance. My beard grew long and unruly. I had long since stopped making records of the plants, spending my time waiting for her to relieve me from my solitude.

A lingering sense that I had forgotten something persisted. For many hours I would pace the forest, thinking hard about what it was, always on the verge of remembering, but then forgetting it once again. Whilst roaming the woods, I chanced upon a huntsman's hut. The remnants

of charcoaled wood still remained where a fire had once been. It was these fragments of human life that made me understand that I had forgotten what it was to have human habits and rituals. I built a fire and the craving for sleep overwhelmed me; the brutal insomnia from which I had been suffering had reduced me to an unthinking shell. I had become inhuman from dwelling in the forest too long and abandoning my work. I longed for rest. Once inside the hut, I unpacked my things and laid them out in a neat row. My compass was missing, but I had no memory of losing it. Delving into my bag, I found the root the old man had given me; I smelt it, still unsure of its purpose. For the first time in months, I rolled out my bedding and the idea of a restful, dream-less sleep seemed possible. No sooner had I closed my eyelids than my love's song weaved its way into my mind.

"Come, my love. Come out and let me see you."

I scrambled to the door and flung it open to see her standing, slightly hidden in the bushes. I ran forward and took her face in my hands. She pulled back as if she had been stung.

"You smell."

I laughed, unsure of what she meant. Repelled, she hung back from me. Confusion and anger dominated her features.

"Your hands. They're repulsive."

I looked at my palms and then the backs of my hands, trying to comprehend what she could mean. Then I remembered.

"Oh, just a root I've been holding."

She stepped back. I pan-icked, stepping after her.

"It's nothing, really."

"It's disgusting."

She turned to leave.

I ran back to the hut and retrieved the root from my bag. I threw it onto the fire. Within seconds, a thick purple smoke rose into the air. It smelt sweet and fragrant, like aniseed and rosehip. I breathed it in and felt revived, my head clear

from fatigue. I turned to her to gain approval, but she had disappeared.

Her anger played on my mind and I once again feared she would not return. I felt sick, at a loss to know how to act. I sat, I stood, I paced the hut. The disgust in her eyes remained with me and brought back thoughts of my father's eyes when I told him of my forest trip and intention to complete my naturalist studies. It mattered not how much I reassured him that it would be for the best and that I would succeed, I could see that I was still a disappointment. I knew I had to prove other-wise to him. For the first few days of her disappearance, I paced in distraction, but after every passing day, I began to sleep better. Feeling rested, I resumed interest in my personal well-being, washed myself, my clothes and shaved. I laughed at seeing my old face revealed in the mirror; it was like being reacquainted with a long-lost friend. Picking up my notebooks, I reviewed the progress I had made so far and was pleased to realize how much I had accomplished. The idea that I would soon be ready to head back to the village began to occupy my thoughts.

After nine days, I was ready to leave the forest. As I was packing up, I found a letter I could not remember having seen before. I'd only brought two of the sweetest of Emily's from the days of our engagement. I knew not how I could have had this letter for so very long without once having espied it in my bag. From the handwriting on the front of the envelope, I knew it was from my father. My heart beat hard as I unfolded the single page. The two lines were written with precision in thick, black ink.

I've tried to love you for my beloved wife's sake, but you have proved yourself worthless. A failure. I would wish you dead but you do not deserve to be reunited with her.

The pain was physical; my chest constricted and I gasped for air. Grabbing at the handle of the hut, I pulled myself up, my limbs heavy, holding me down, each movement a struggle. I stumbled outside, trying to breathe the forest air. Crisp, clean light illuminated the clearing, I turned and she was standing behind me with her small hand outstretched.

"Stay here with me now."

Her song vibrated into my soul anew, drawing me to her. She sang of comfort, love and home, only now I could comprehend the words and they were a welcome salve. This time she did not trick me; I kissed her first. I took her into my arms and pressed my lips against hers in an act that was both tender and violent.

The forest was once again beautiful, gleaming; it shone, accepting me as one of its own. I was protected. My father had betrayed his lawful son and heir, an act unnatural amongst both the wild and the civilized; I no longer had anything to prove

to him. The happiness I had felt on first hearing her song flooded back through my veins and warmed my body and soul. Oh happiness, home and joy! But, even at that moment of reanimation, I had the creeping sense that I had felt this kind of cruel comfort before. The temporary suspension of pain and loneliness, forced out by an external invading force that I had sought and was to be my downfall.

The days were short again, and it was cold. No snow had yet fallen. The moments I was with her, I experienced a thousand emotions in the space of a few seconds: relief, lust, tenderness, calm, frustration and anger. And then she would leave me, a man more abandoned and lonely than ever. She came and went at her whim; I never knew at what time she would come or how long she would stay. I got a sense of being controlled, part of a larger game, where the rules were set by an unknown force and entirely incomprehensible to the players. Longing for her to come, I would shout into the forest; the trees watched, silent, keeping guard.

Sleeping and eating were impossible. Desperation was the only thing I felt when we were parted. The sense of forest as home had long faded, revived for shorter and shorter periods when she arrived, her face benevolent and kind as an angel, but with the lustful eye of a devil. I begged her to soothe me to sleep while she was there, knowing that once she departed, I would sit for hours staring into the woods, listening and watching for her return. She would feed me, laughing at my hunger and calling me her "little one", as if a child waiting to be nourished from its mother's breast. I cried and she would rock me back and forth, sing her song of home, and for those brief moments I was home once again. I had lost my will and lived only for the nourishment she gave me.

Sitting alone, staring into my campfire, I became aware of a figure I could see from the corner of my eye. When I turned my head to look, there was nothing there, only the trees, but I continued to see him, feel his presence, hear his breath. This marginal figure haunted me for days, driving me to distraction. He lingered like a piece of grit, scratching my eye and impairing my vision. I wandered through the woods, listening to the sounds, cocking my ear, as a cat would to identify danger. By this time, I was again unshaven, unclean and animalistic in my habits, sniffing the air and waiting for the wind to change to get a better sense of what was happening around me. My brief moments of sleep were in her arms, and continued dread and anxiety plagued me when we were apart. I survived always on edge—waiting, waiting, waiting—and then in a trice responding, going into flight at the barest environmental change. I would run through the woods and stop only to

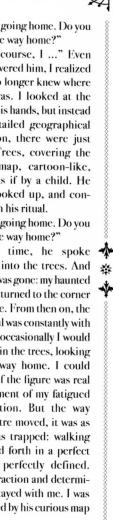

smell the air for predators. This was when I saw the figure in full: a man of about thirty years of age, although from his unkempt appearance this was difficult to discern exactly. His clothes were shredded and his hair and beard bedraggled. He stood staring into the trees and for long moments at a time he'd stay fixed in one spot and then pace, as if in an invisible cage, back and forth about three feet in distance. He would then stop again and stare, take what looked like a map from his pocket, look down at it, pull at his hair and look around in a panic, as if lost.

"Hello!" I shouted, as loud as I could. He took no notice of me and performed his ritual over again. I shouted again and ran to him, but he didn't look up or even seem to notice me. "Are you lost?"

He continued his routine. Pulling the map from his pocket, looking at it and then grasping his hair in despair and terror. Without looking up he said:

"I'm going home. Do you know the way home?"

"Of course, I ..." Even as I answered him, I realized that I no longer knew where home was. I looked at the map in his hands, but instead of a detailed geographical depiction, there were just trees. Trees, covering the entire map, cartoon-like, drawn as if by a child. He never looked up, and continued in his ritual.

"I'm going home. Do you know the way home?"

This time, he spoke directly into the trees. And then he was gone: my haunted figure returned to the corner of my eye. From then on, the poor soul was constantly with me, and occasionally I would see him in the trees, looking for his way home. I could not tell if the figure was real or a figment of my fatigued imagination. But the way my spectre moved, it was as if he was trapped: walking back and forth in a perfect square, perfectly defined. His distraction and determination stayed with me. I was perplexed by his curious map

of trees that showed no other landmarks or features. It was with panic that I remembered my missing compass, the enclosed forest and short winter days. He would never find his way back home.

barest thread of an image of the players on the stage. An impression of laughter, fear and joy left me, as did the idea that there was another place I could not get to. Too tired to run, my anticipation or interest in my surroundings evaporated. I no longer held any clear sense that she or my surroundings were real; everything merged into a mass of indistinguishable impressions and fleeting images. The only thing that was clear was a longing for her, a longing that lived in every part of my mind, imagination and body. Everything had been obscured and consigned to a dream world that existed behind a glass wall, visible but impenetrable.

The lonely ghost

So exhausted was I by this time that I felt that I was fading away, depleted, my past hopes and aspirations gone. The memory of civilization was just a dream: like a play I had seen in childhood and only had the

I was freezing when I awoke. It was with horror I saw I was naked and alone.

Curious map of trees

What had I come to, my shame evident before me? I shuddered with cold and with desperation at my situation. Disgusted with myself, I looked about for my clothing and dressed in haste, all the while knowing I wanted more and would let her take control of me again and again, without end, until all that was left was my longing to be satiated by her. I cried tears of frustration at my own weakness. I was in the hands of an external force—a force I had turned to thinking it was a release from my loneliness, but that had trapped me in a world of ghoulish nightmares. The love that

I thought I had found had become an obsession and was now a tyranny. I'd mistaken an addiction to sin for love. Her face from the previous night's passion lingered before me, distorted, twisted into a lustful determination, her beauty and calm gone. She screamed the unearthly cry of a fox coupling in the dead of night. The sound of her still reverberated all about me, vibrating through my brain and permeating me as her seductive forest song had done before.

The falseness of my position was all of a sudden clear. If I stayed in the woods and gave in to my addiction, I would die her slow death, perished from cold and hunger. I had to find the strength and fortitude to fight for my life—escape from the woods and the creature who kept me there.

In panic I ran; my intention was to leave the forest immediately, caring not for provisions or protection, such was my haste. From my knowledge of the woods, I thought I would be able to find a path soon enough and get on my way. I bitterly regretted the loss of my compass, but at least I was confident I could follow the sun during daylight. As the sun began to set, my hope also sank with it. I wandered desperately. Looking into the mass of trees, I paced, trying to work out which way I had come and which way I needed to go. The light faded, tricking me to see branches as the limbs of half-hidden men, and hearing in the call of birds the sneering laughter of hunters. Faint with exhaustion, pushing forward, I half ran through the trees, the cackling birds taunting me, shapes in the trees mutated into the forest woman's lustful distorted image, mocking and merciless. I cried.

"I want to go home."

At this, the trees sighed in unison and a path opened up before me. The branches of the trees pinned back and intertwined to create a beautiful and elaborate arch. As I walked forward, the branches closed behind me. I stumbled on and, within what seemed like a few moments, I was back at my huntsman's hut, shepherded there by her arboreal accomplices. I knew not whether to rejoice or shudder. It was her will that I should be brought back to this spot, brought back after being taught a lesson: the forest was now my prison.

In haste, I collected my things together, determined that I would not be imprisoned, contained like a beast. As I packed my books into my bag, one fell to the ground and lay open. The page was clean. I grabbed the book and I scanned page after page; they were

all empty. Rushing outside, I ran into the trees, looking for the species that I had discovered, which had been so abundant, but they too were all gone.

There was one plant I knew to be real. The root the old man had given me. I remembered how revitalized I had felt when inhaling its smoke. How after a few days, I had felt rested and strong, and the hold that she had over me had lessened. Was I exchanging one drug for another: her primitive love for an equally primitive barbiturate? I had no choice; I was desperate for anything that gave me even the smallest hope of escape. I crawled through the bracken, searching, groping. I pulled up plant after plant, inspecting the roots, but these plants were all known to me. Twilight took hold. My ghost crept from the shadow of my vision and then I saw him up ahead, standing as before at the edge of the clearing, looking into the trees.

"Do you know the way home?"

I heard him say it and then he continued his pacing up and down in a line. I approached him. He took his map from his pocket and looked at it. I tried to speak but was unable. He turned and walked into the trees. I was left standing there, but something shone in the twilight. I bent down to pick it up and, in my direct eye line, emerged an unusual plant. I pulled it free from the ground. The root exposed was of the type I'd been desperately seeking.

With mixed feelings, I lit the pipe. The purple smoke rose into the air and filled the hut. Immediately, I felt revived. Human life once again flooded into my cheeks, my strength returned and I grew hungry, but my only thought was of freedom.

I knew that she would try and stop me, and I would be powerless against her unless I was strong and resolute. She commanded the forest, the trees were her servants. How would I get free, how could I protect myself from her song? Dejected, I searched and found Emily's prayer book. I kissed it. Reading through the words, I found the strength in God's revelation. Mr. Darwin was wrong. The devil did exist; I had met her, loved her and shared my bed with her. The same God who made Man also created the devils that frequented the earth. If God created the demons to tempt us from our civilized ways, then He would also send us the Grace by which to escape them. And those who wished to be saved, could be.

My faith renewed, I watched the purple smoke rising from my pipe; my memory of her reaction to it returned. It was a connection I hadn't made, my mind being so confused from her influence. She had recoiled from its smell and then been absent for many days, giving me time to recover my mind and strength. What if the root not only revived those under the influence of this foul forest creature, but repelled it too? I couldn't be sure how much impact it

would have, but I was sure it would be enough for me to get away. The root was a godsend.

I had enough of the plant for two pipes. I had already lit one. I couldn't be sure when she might appear and I had to be ready; the second pipe was my only hope. Grabbing the prayer book, I held it to my chest and began to recite the Lord's Prayer. It fortified me and gave me hope I would once again see Emily and England. I had but a few things and I left anything unnecessary. It was then that I remembered by lost compass. My resolve flagged again but I sang; I sang the song I had on my lips when I had first come to the forest: "Dear Lord and Father of Mankind". My voice rose almost to a shout.

Breathe through the heats
of our desire
Thy coolness and Thy
balm;
Let sense be dumb, let
flesh retire;
Speak through the

*earthquake,
wind, and fire,
O still, small voice
of calm.*

It was then that the forest once again began to vibrate and a light glowed through the hut window. I was not sure that my guess about the root would be correct, but either I would escape... or stay and die. Preparing myself for the inevitable encounter, I inhaled deeply on the pipe and, as I opened the door,

Mysterious root

her silhouette stepped from the trees into the clearing of the camp. The trees closed their branches behind her, the entire enclosure becoming a prison as the branches intertwined, making a dense, impenetrable wall. They bent their tops to obscure light from above, the darkness overbearing and oppressive as if there was an oncoming storm.

"My friends tell me you're planning to leave us." I stared

at her, holding my breath. "I thought you were happy here in your new forest home." I held out my hand to her. She cocked her head, looking at me quizzically, sniffed the air and frowned. I kept walking forward, until I came eye to eye with her. I grabbed her around her waist and kissed her, she relaxed in my arms, awaiting a lover's kiss. I exhaled the smoke directly into her lungs. An unholy scream rang through the

woods; every tree, plant and animal had been scorched. She recoiled, as did the trees, their branches no longer a barrier. Writhing, her body convulsed; her distorted face changing through a thousand different images, the features of my father and Emily passed across her visage. I ran into the woods, not daring to look back at what might follow. I kept going until the darkness surrounded me. Snow began to fall, the light flakes resting on all they touched. I collapsed.

As I opened my eyes, a light dazzled me. She had caught up with me. How could I ever imagine I'd be safe? I lifted my head and it was heavy under the weight of snow that had fallen whilst I was unconscious. Snow covered everything, the branches of the trees coated as if wearing a new, clean set of clothes. The forest was silent. The vibration of the forest song began to emerge, muffled under the burden of snow. The light approached. I struggled from the ground, the snow and my fatigue slowing me. Fear pulsed through my body, but my limbs were heavy, leaden as in a nightmare. Her voice was penetrating my mind with promises of eternal peace; the song grew louder and the light brighter. Then another sound joined the forest music from the opposite direction: the bark of a dog. I saw something black, loping, approaching through the trees, and directly behind, three lights, a few feet apart, weaving through the undergrowth. I ran with all my strength towards the weak lights of the men, stumbling as I went, my knees partially giving way beneath me. Her voice grew louder and I wanted to turn back and come under her protection, give up my life and die a slow but oblivious death. A black Labrador jumped up at me, and knocked me backwards. As I turned, attempting to get back to my feet, the forest woman was upon me, her benevolent face looking down, full of the promise of an easy death. The dog growled at her. I held out my hand to her and she looked down with love and gratitude. Just as our fingers were to touch, the first man emerged through the trees. He held his burning torch in front of him. A sweet smelling, purple smoke rose from the flames.

"Get back," he warned, walking forward with his torch.

"I've always been good to huntsmen. Leave this one for me." She was hunkered down, lowering herself as a cat does when threatened with danger.

"He is foolish, he doesn't understand." He then addressed me. "Get up, come here and stand behind me." I did as the man said. The dog walked alongside me. As I reached him, I collapsed to my knees.

"Now leave us be," the hunter commanded. The light and music stopped. She had gone.

Even though I've tried hard to remember what happened in the following weeks, it was little more than a haze. I had a fever, barely waking, barely sleeping: nightmares of running in the forest, coming up against impenetrable walls, the branches containing and controlling me. When the fever finally left, the villagers nursed me back to health and little by little I regained my strength.

Arriving back in London was a great joy when I saw Emily waiting for me on the platform. She looked pale and thin but just as beautiful as ever. We are now the best of friends; at first I was crestfallen, hoping she would come back to me, but her friendship is tender and kind and much love is shared between us. It is the purest form of love, unsullied by base actions. She has helped me with my newfound cause. Since my escape from the forest and second chance at a real life, I write. This pamphlet is one of the fruits of my endeavours to help those who are lonely, dejected and unloved. I wish to raise their spirits so they can protect themselves from all the evils of the world: drugs, drink, prostitution; the things that one turns to when the heart is not whole. If you cannot give and accept charity then no one can save you. We have to learn to love one another, develop understanding and kindness. Without that, we are lost. Heed my warning friends: allow charity into your life and return it in full without restraint or resistance. Christ preached it, God offers it, and the best of our world depends on it. It is the only hope we have.

It would be wrong to say I do not still struggle with my feelings of failure and loneliness. This is my cross to bear. Father persists in his coldness towards me despite my entreaties to heal our wounds and become a loving father to his son. My forest ghost haunts me still; I see him in the corner of my eye and I am grateful, both that he delivered me and that he provides a constant reminder that the torment I suffered was entirely real. Sometimes when I sleep, I hear the song of the Skogsrå, for that is the

creature's name. I now know the nature of the beast. It is the untamed primitiveness of a world without God's Grace. She calls me back to my forest prison and it is only with the full strength of my God-supported will, and the love of Emily, that I do not run to her.

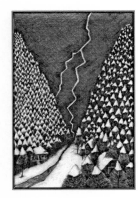

THE
HEART OF A HEARTLESS WORLD
OR
SUPERNATURAL TERRORS
AT THE HEART OF THE FOREST

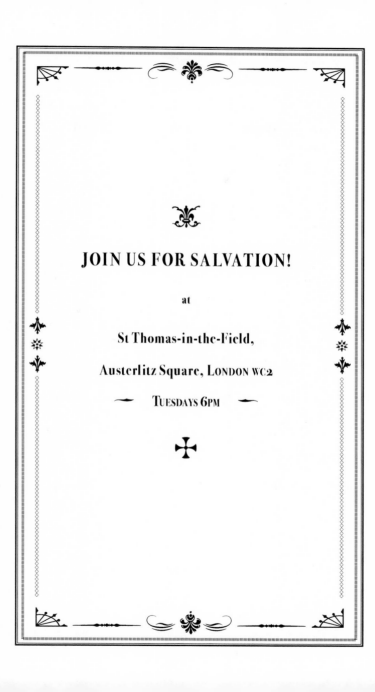

JOIN US FOR SALVATION!

at

St Thomas-in-the-Field,

Austerlitz Square, LONDON WC2

TUESDAYS 6PM

KILLING RACHEL

The music was loud. People laughed, mouthing the words of "Rolling in the Deep" at one another. A woman danced on the table, holding her drink high like a sacrificial goblet. It swayed with the music, the liquid threatening to leap from the glass onto the heads of spectators.

"Get this down your neck." Belinda, a work friend, pushed a shot into Rachel's hand. Rachel checked for the emergency exits. There were four. Her nearest was next to the bar. How could anyone get out of here in an emergency? Any hesitation from the security staff and it would be another Bradford disaster. Rachel could see the headlines: FIFTY-SIX DIE IN NIGHTCLUB INFERNO.

She sank backwards into the leather sofa; it consumed her, sucking her in. A drunken couple fell across her, kissing with wide mouths and visible tongues. Jimmy lifted his hand, placing it on the top of her head. Her ears flinched at each beat of the music. As it merged with the sounds of human exhilaration it deadened into silence. Sweat dripped down her back; she wanted to wipe it away as she breathed deeper and deeper, struggling for air. She felt dizzy, small sparkly dots leaping up and down before her eyes. Jimmy pulled her backwards, downwards. Gravity suckled her body, sapping its essence. She wanted to cry out, knowing the sound would only be absorbed into the darkness, cherished greedily by the void. The hand clamped about her skull, an even application of pressure wrapping itself around her brain, careful caresses that gently squeezed. No fixed point, freefalling, body limp, devoid of purpose. The hand tightened its hold, her eyes dimmed, the light-particles increased as her heart pounded ever more harshly, a hard thump violently clashing with an intense but deep pulse. The abyss devoured her. She gasped for any breath it permitted her to make: shallow, short, desperate. The light extinguished, the sound and silence crushed her. The couple were an indistinguishable outline, blending and fading to blackness as Rachel's body lost power. She tried to stand but fell to the floor. Crawling forward, she grasped a pair of legs.

"Help me. Please. Help me."

Rachel opened her eyes. The room was white; its brightness made it difficult to see any details. The bed was comfortable and warm. Confusion flooded her mind. What was she doing in bed, a bed she didn't know, in a place she didn't recognise? A club, she'd been in a club. Realisation dawned: this must be a hospital ward. She was relieved. At last she'd had an attack someone had taken seriously. Now she'd get a diagnosis. All those who doubted her would be sorry.

"A trick of the mind," that doctor at the Accident and Emergency had said. But temporarily losing her sight had led her to expect a brain tumour at the very least. Or even Mad Cow Disease, which would definitely be her mum's fault for feeding her all those cheap burgers as a kid. What a show she'd put on. Snivelling and blubbing like a baby, she'd made the nurse stay with her, holding her hand while she recounted every last detail of her health fears. "I can give you something to reduce your anxiety," the doctor had offered, poised to write a prescription. She didn't need drugs; she just needed to know what was wrong with her.

On leaving the hospital Rachel had marched straight into the nurse.

"Glad to see you're still alive. Take it easy," the nurse mocked. If only she could see Rachel now.

Her eyes began to adjust to the light. The room was beautifully decorated in Regency style. Being an interior designer, Rachel was used to seeing period interpretations, but this was perfect. It was no NHS room. This must be an exclusive private establishment to be decorated in such a grand manner.

However, it was a strange hospital that had pictures of Death decorating its walls. All four images showed personifications of Death. The first was of a delicate young boy. Underneath it read: *Hellenic, Thanatos.* The next, *Hindu, King Yama or King of Karmic Justice*, depicted a figure riding a black buffalo and carrying a rope lasso. A feminine skeletal form wearing a crown and surrounded by flowers was called *La Santa Muerte* or *Saint Death*. Finally, the figure of *The Grim Reaper* stared down at her. Death was carrying a large scythe and clothed in a black cloak and hood. Rachel wondered how many variations there could be: as many as there were belief systems, possibly.

She heard the door handle slowly being turned and stared at the door. It suddenly flung open, banged against the wall and deflected back into its frame, smacking the person on the threshold. For a flash, Rachel saw a figure all in black and heard a grunt of pain. Another moment passed. The door now gently began to open. Emerging from behind it was a young man. Slim and tall, his skin so pale it was touched with blue, his brow knotted above black eyes, he edged forward with small steps, stopping and pulling at his robe as if it were snagged on a branch. He held out his right hand. Rachel stared, looking from his right hand to his left: the left was much larger. Jimmy flushed red, withdrew it, and placed his enlarged hand behind his back.

"I'm afraid you're dead." He mumbled it, refusing to meet her eyes.

"Dead?"

"Yeah, dead." He nodded.

"Really? Dead?" Rachel looked at her hands, and down at her body. "I don't feel dead. You sure?" She was grabbing parts of her body.

"Well, in-limbo dead." It sounded like an apology.

"Limbo dead?" Rachel screwed up her nose.

"I'm afraid there's been a terrible mistake." He looked to the floor and again blushed.

*****

"Tea?" Jimmy asked as he hovered the teapot above the delicate china cup and saucer set in front of her.

"Erm, yes please." Rachel watched as the liquid filled her cup. She looked up at Jimmy and watched his face, serious as he concentrated on his task.

"Milk? Sugar?" he enquired.

"No, sweet enough. So what was it in the end?" She stared at him, raising her eyebrows.

"In the end?" Jimmy had no idea what she meant. He was also unused to being glared at by an attractive young woman. How was he expected to think under such circumstances? She didn't wait for his reply.

"Brain tumour? Thrombosis? No, no, no, let me guess, it must have been a stroke." He frowned and put down the teapot.

"I told you it was a mis ..." He stopped.

"A 'mis'? A 'mis' what?" She was impatient.

"A mysterious type of stroke, that was it." He nodded. "Yes, that was definitely it."

"I knew it!" Almost shouting, she knocked the table as she stood up. Tea splashed into the saucer. "I knew there was something wrong. I bet they're all sorry now." Her glee was alarming to Jimmy. He'd never seen someone so happy to be dead.

"'They'? Who are 'they'?" He was confused.

"Family, friends, doctors. You know, anyone who didn't believe me." She'd shown them they were all wrong by up and dying on them. They'd be sorry now! And at last, maintaining her exhausting pretence of "successful young woman in control of her life" was over. She breathed a sigh of relief.

"Oh, I see. Yes, well, sorry, but not in the way you mean, I guess." Her zeal overwhelmed him.

"And you're 'The Caretaker' and you look after those who come to live in limbo?"

"Erm, yes, sorry, you'll have to put up with me for the time being." His laugh was nervous, and he shrugged his shoulders, raising his eyebrows as he spoke.

"And I'm in limbo because it hasn't been decided by the powers that be, whoever they are, what's going to happen to me?"

"Yes, right again." Coughing slightly, he concentrated on replacing his cup into its saucer.

"How come I'm in limbo? Where will I go? How long will it take?" Her familiar vertigo rose. Death was beginning to make less sense than life.

Her knowledge of afterlife options was limited. She was not religious and didn't believe in God, or rather not the Christian god presented to her as a child. School assembly, when they'd all mumbled the Lord's Prayer and sang a handful of hymns, was the nearest she'd come to any kind of worship. Fluffy

clouds with cherubs lounging around, playing miniature harps was the limit of her imagination. And
then she considered the alternative. Naked people
tied to stakes, fire licking up their bodies, their
screams piercing and desperate. She shuddered.

"Don't worry, it will be okay." He tried to smile.

"That's not really an answer, is it?" Confusion
and uncertainty seemed to permeate both sides of
the divide.

"Well, no, yes, but …"

This girl was going to be troublesome. She had
been such a diligent anxiety sufferer for him, one
of his better clients really; he'd had no idea she'd be
so assertive. Death's Scythe hadn't worked how he'd
imagined, and now he was stuck with her until he
could work out how to finish the job he'd started,
without Death finding out his intention to keep killing. Or discovering Rachel before he entirely killed
her. How he was going to keep her quiet, hiding her
in Death's house, he wasn't yet sure.

Purveyor of panic attacks, red mists and black dogs.
Jimmy sighed and replaced his business card into
his wallet.

"A lot of good it does me. It's all right for you.
People look up to you: they respect and fear you.
But me, they think they've a physical ailment, trying
to give their miseries a tangible cause. All my good

work wasted." Jimmy stared into his china teacup, his shoulders hunched forward causing his black robe to fall down about the tops of his arms. He sat in one of two wing back chairs that were positioned in front of the iron fireplace. Death's study was elegant, if modelled on a Sherlock Holmes Victoriana. Book shelves were lined with leather-bound editions and the walls adorned with red-wine flock paper.

Death sat next to Jimmy, perched on the arm of the chair. His slender fingers curled around his shoulders. "Look Jimmy, you do a really important job, and you're good at it. You remind people of their fallibility, that life is at times ... let's say ... difficult, and pain is inevitable. Because of the misery you bring, people understand happiness when it comes to them. Because of your pain, they value the goodness in life. There cannot be one without the other. You are necessary for humanity to be human."

"That's not true and you know it. I'm just something to be swept under the carpet. No one brags about the amazing panic attacks or the feelings of utter hopelessness they just experienced. It's just not the done thing."

Death picked up his cup and sat in the chair opposite to Jimmy. "Wonderful blend of tea by the way. What about the suicides? There's something to think about."

"No, it's not. Where's the nobility in that? It's not quite the same as dying after a long, brave fight with cancer. That has romance. I'm just not useful, glamorous or imposing. I'm an embarrassment."

"That's not true, Jimmy. Everyone here has a crucial role and you really are doing a fantastic job. There are people living with terrible depressions across the globe and all thanks to you. Why can't you just be yourself? You'll make yourself ill trying to be something you're not, and, if the robe fits ..." Death glanced at his brother's sagging garment and continued, "Your sisters are happy with their jobs."

"That might be something to do with them being spirits of violent death. Battle, accident and murder are so much juicier than suicide."

"Juicy, yes, ah, I see. Anyway, this is what you were created to do. Give it time, you may come to enjoy it again. If not, I'll put a word in for you, see if we can't get your duties expanded a little."

"Really? Would you? I'd be so grateful, Jules. And I'd love a scythe like yours." Jimmy pretended to cut through the air with his imaginary scythe.

"We've been through this. The Scythe of Death is a unique tool. What's wrong with your enlarged hand, anyway? Jolly dandy, I've always thought, and at least you don't have the burden of carrying a scythe around. Now, I want to hear no more about this until you've given it your best effort. Off you go."

As the door closed on Jimmy, Jules sighed in frustration. He wondered how long it would take for Jimmy to confess his "mistake".

Limbo consisted of two rooms. When she'd imagined being dead she certainly didn't foresee being confined to a bedroom and living room and treated like a pampered prisoner. Jimmy jumped at every noise and kept the doors locked. Standing at the large French windows, she stared out into the garden. The garden was serene and reminded her of those she'd seen on visits to English stately homes. Roses of pink, yellow and crimson red framed the doorway, and beyond a small patio were rows of intricately crafted topiary. In the distance she could see the top of a large domed glasshouse. Rachel tried the door handles. Locked. But then, she knew that already.

"Er, herm, Rachel, it's your turn." Jimmy was sitting at the table. In front of him was a Scrabble board. He was smiling.

"I just put down 'DEAD'. It was worth six points. Not too bad, I think you'll admit." He was nodding, pleased with himself. Rachel looked at the board.

"I guess it's okay, but if you had laid it the other way you could have got the triple word score." Jimmy stopped smiling. His eyes darted from one part of the board to the other.

"Where?" He continued searching as Rachel picked up her counters and covered a triple word score.

"You just don't think it through, Jimmy. Strategy isn't your strong point and your poker face is terrible." Rachel affected the smug head tilt of a winner.

"See, 'DEATH'." Mumbling numbers, she calculated her score. "Twenty-seven points. There you go, that's how to play the game." She laughed. This was the first time she'd played board games and loved it. When alive she'd never made time for games. If it wasn't about her career then she hadn't bothered, not being able to see the point. Games were fun. But Jimmy lashed out, pushing the board away from him. Counters slid across the smooth surface and came to rest, creating yet to be discovered words.

"How's that for strategy?" He folded his arms and turned his head away.

"You'll never win if you don't have a plan."

He snorted. "Well, maybe that's your problem: you're too cold and calculating."

"What do you mean by that?" Rachel was surprised.

"With all your plans and schemes, there's no room to enjoy yourself."

"What?! You're 'The Caretaker' and you're

supposed to look after me, but all we've done is play Scrabble and you ALWAYS get upset 'cause I ALWAYS win. And I still have no idea what I'm doing in limbo and what's going to happen to me. Under the circumstances, I think I'm pretty relaxed."

"What did you expect? It *is* limbo."

"I didn't expect it to be like an eternal Christmas afternoon playing Scrabble with my bad loser of a little brother." They were both standing up, facing each other.

"You're just like my brother – I try really hard and you don't appreciate me." Jimmy grabbed a handful of tiles and threw them into the box where they bounced in all directions. "I don't know why I bother." He reached forward and scraped the escapee letters towards himself. The stress of keeping Rachel a secret and maintaining his regular duties was beginning to play havoc with his nerves.

Rachel smiled. "Now you sound like my mother."

"At least you have a mother." Jimmy kept his gaze fixed on a tile marked with the letter S, tears welling in his eyes.

Rachel started to laugh. "Oh Jimmy, I'm sorry." She touched him on the hand. He pulled it away slowly, leaving her finger resting on the S.

"Okay. Apology accepted." He looked at her from lowered lids. Rachel bounded up to him.

"Why don't we go out? I think we need it. We're going to go crazy locked up in here. And it's only been four days."

"I don't think so." He avoided her eager stare.

"Oh Jimmy, why not?" He couldn't risk Jules seeing them. "Please, please, please. I'll teach you how to beat me at chess and Scrabble. Strategy will be your middle name." She looked up at him with pleading eyes.

"Oh alright, but you must do as I say, and get out of sight if need be. Understand?"

The sky was clear and blue. It was enormous and stretched for eternity. To Rachel, it was like the Sunday afternoon skies when she had been a child, and the sun was yellow and hot and kept her warm even without a cardigan. Gravel crunched under her feet and she wanted to ask Jimmy if they could have an ice-cream. It would complete her picture of a perfect summer's afternoon: a memory formed before her father had gone away. Plants climbed the garden walls, creating protective layers from the outside world – whatever the world outside of limbo might be. Green surrounded them, with dots of colour dripping from each stem or branch. It was sumptuous. She felt calm with a peace that she rarely knew. Limbo was so bland that it rendered any of her fears unfounded, and her quiet routine of games and chats was eroding her sharp edges. If this was death, then nothing else bad could happen to her. She no longer needed to prove herself to anyone.

Jimmy towered over her, and it was as if she was walking next to nobody with his head so far above hers. Rachel watched him for a moment. He could have been made from a "how to build the ideal human kit" – except that something in the assembly had gone awry. If he hadn't been so extreme in opposites, he would be beautiful. But his eyes were a little too dark and his cheeks a little too sharp. His too pale skin accentuated his too chiselled face. And he shuffled, round-shouldered, as if he knew he was the remaindered version of a man, a blurred photocopy of the template. He kept his enlarged hand behind his back and pointed with the other.

"That's the *Gallica* or Rose of Provins."

Hanging from the wall were a huddle of deep-pink roses whose fine petals layered and curled into one another.

"Very pretty." Leaning in, she tried to smell them but stumbled forward. He caught hold of her arm with his enlarged hand.

"It's usually me that falls." He giggled, embarrassed as he set her on her feet, and withdrew his hand, placing it behind his back. He continued.

"They're often called The Apothecary's Rose, *R. gallica officinalis*, and were grown in the Middle

Ages in monastic herbaria for their alleged medicinal properties. They eventually became famous in English history as the Red Rose of Lancaster." His laugh was nervous. "Or so I've heard." He blushed.

"Wow, I'm impressed. I don't know anything about flowers and trees. Interiors are more my area." Rachel thought of her flat. It was immaculate, beautiful. She'd designed it herself with exacting care. Months of agonising debate, years of intense mental visualisation. Colour schemes, fabrics, flooring. All designed to balance light and mood to reflect her unique character and image.

"You're like my brother. He loves to decorate, he's always at it. That's why the house is immaculate. I prefer nature. It's just so ..." Unable to think of the word, he frowned and fell silent for a moment. Then repeated, "It's just so."

"'Just so'? Don't you mean 'just is'?" Rachel screwed up her nose.

"No, I don't. For example, there are over a hundred types of roses and thousands of cultivars. And they're all perfect. They have a place and a function that fits with the rest of nature. It just works."

"But the advantage with decorating is creating perfection yourself. I'm in total control when I design a room: I decide on everything and make it happen. Nothing is overlooked and that's all down to me."

"That's a very limited idea of perfection."

Rachel scrutinised him. This was a very different Jimmy than the one who threw Scrabble pieces around the room.

"I need to show you something." He walked to the exit and stuck his head out, looking both ways before leading her through the doorway. Bobbing her head down to avoid the roses that hung from the frame, she followed him. In front was the entrance to a huge glasshouse. It stood at least 200 feet high, and reminded her of the top part of the club from a suit of cards. An ornate cast iron spire reached into the sky, as if to pop clouds. Hundreds, maybe even thousands of these glasshouses lined the path, shrinking as they receded into the distance.

"Bloody hell." Rachel was flabbergasted. She'd only ever seen one glasshouse at a time and it was impressive enough on its own. Jimmy nodded, smiling.

"Why on earth – or in limbo – are there so many?"

"Where else do you think all the plant life that has ever existed is kept?" Jimmy brimmed with satisfaction.

"To be fair, Jimmy, I've never thought about it before. I just assumed they'd be on earth and gone forever when, you know, they died."

"It's amazing, isn't it?" He gestured with arms

wide. "You can find anything you want, from any point in history."

"But how? There's so many of them." Bright beams reflected on the glass. Shielding her eyes from the glare, she stared up the path towards the receding buildings.

Jimmy beamed with pride again. "The Gardener is very good with databases, as well as plants. This is one of my faves." He beckoned her along as he marched down the path. Rachel followed, half running behind him, curious at what Jimmy was so excited to share with her.

"How much longer?" Rachel whined, stopping to remove a stone from her shoe.

"You were nagging to get outside, now you're moaning about being out."

"My feet hurt in these shoes. I just don't have the right footwear for this."

"Here we are." Jimmy stopped in front of a glasshouse and pointed to a sign. Rachel read it aloud.

"Fungi, English, Extinct 1820–2015." Placing his hands on the brass handles, Jimmy pushed open the doors.

Musty with the richness of moist earth, the smell was overwhelming. Rachel stood in the middle of a British woodland. Trees reached up to the roof, deep-green ferns spread across the ground, and fungi of all types bred between mosses. The light was dim and the air damp. They were completely insulated. Misshapen growths twisted from tree trunks, and toadstools that could have been conjured by fairies huddled together around her feet. She laughed.

"It's like pixieland." Nature had created a messy and gnarled form of perfection. Rachel thought it beautiful.

Jimmy bent down and pulled back some fern leaves. Beneath was a cluster of bright-purple domes, small white blotches spread over their curves.

"These are *Cortinarius cumatilis*. They became extinct in 1868." Rachel bent down beside him.

"They're incredible." She smiled at Jimmy.

"Yes they are, and just think, you'd never have seen them if you hadn't come here." He stood up and put his hands on his hips. "Over 70 varieties of fungi have become extinct in the UK during the last 200 years."

"How do you know all of this? It's impressive, Jimmy. You're rubbish at Scrabble, but you're magic at this stuff." Jimmy glowed red and grinned.

"The Gardener is a friend of mine, and she lets me help out a bit. I find it relaxing." Rachel watched him as he wandered further into the wood.

"It's more than that, Jimmy." She followed him,

tottering amongst the fungi, wobbling as she placed one foot in front of the other. He shouted without looking back.

"Watch out for the large pink one on your left. *Hygrophorus russula* or Pinkmottle Woodwax, extinct 1903. She's quite a beauty."

As she followed Jimmy further into the woods, she noticed the walls of the glasshouse had ceased to contain them, and they seamlessly merged and became a large wood. Instead of fungi, small blue flowers were sprouting from the ground. Blue overtook green until the entire floor of the wood was smothered in small violet-blue bells.

"Everything is always okay in the woods." Jimmy was staring down at the flowers.

"Yes, it is," she said. They stood in silence for a moment. Speaking with Jimmy was easy; she felt no need to impress him or fear of saying the wrong thing.

"So why doesn't your brother appreciate you when you're part of all this?"

Jimmy turned away from her and then shrugged.

"All this isn't my job and all Jules is interested in is duty." He wouldn't face her.

"He doesn't see what you're capable of, thinks you're young and idiotic, and your feelings count for nothing?" Her mum didn't even make an attempt at concealing this was how she felt about Rachel. Nipping to Ikea and throwing a few matching cushions on the sofa was her mother's idea of interior design. Art college was an expensive indulgence, according to her. She never realised how hard Rachel had worked at college and to get her first break. The harder Rachel worked, the less it counted.

Jimmy's lips tugged upwards at her sarcasm.

"Yes, I suppose. Don't get me wrong, I love him and all that. He looks after me, sort of, and I respect what he does ... he's awfully efficient." Jimmy stopped.

"But?" Rachel walked towards him, trying to get a better look at his expression.

"But, he doesn't understand my job. At all. It's okay for him, he's the big cheese around here and in the Living World, no one has any choice but to obey him, but nobody respects what I do. It's just not cool." He stooped down and plucked a flower from the top of its stem. A love god, or god of war, anything would be better than being the god of petty miseries.

"They're endangered, you know." Rachel smiled. Jimmy looked into the palm of his hand, bewildered.

"Oh, yes. Of course, silly me." He frowned.

"They're not here." Rachel grinned at him.

"It was a joke, I see, yes." They smiled at one another.

"So you're sad because you're not cool?" Rachel asked. Jimmy stared at her.

"Yes, no, of course not. I'd like more responsibility but he never listens. I never seem to do enough to impress him; I only ever disappoint him." Jimmy sighed.

"Well, I think you're doing a good job of looking after me. I'd never have seen all this –" Rachel spun around and stopped directly in front of Jimmy, "– if you hadn't shown it to me." Jimmy glowed with pleasure and then shrugged and shook his head and turned away.

"But it's not ..." He stumbled into silence again, he couldn't tell her what he really did.

"Is that why you're embarrassed of your hand? Being less than perfect isn't cool?" Looking at the tiny crushed flower in his palm, he ignored her.

"This is *Hyacinthoides non-scripta*. It was named after Hyacinth, lover of the god Apollo. As Hyacinth lay dying, this flower sprang from his blood. Apollo marked the petals with his tears of grief and the marks spelled the word, 'alas'."

"That's so sad." She listened to the wood pigeon cooing its rhythmic song. "You know, Jimmy, I think being good at board games is over-rated."

*****

Jimmy waited for a moment and listened. He couldn't hear anything. Jules should be having his nap at this time. Satisfied he wouldn't be interrupted, he gently lifted the brass catch and pulled the cabinet door open. The Scythe was nestled in its black velvet cradle. It was an awe-inspiring object. He'd thought through all the alternatives. Jimmy considered asking his sisters, but they were mean and would probably tell Jules. They told him everything. And he knew he had to go through with the job he'd started. Taking Rachel back home would be an anti-climax. And she did seem pleased to be dead.

Grabbing the Scythe, he turned it in the air, dropped it to ground level and began to mow from left to right. It floated, perfectly balanced. Jimmy spun around, holding the Scythe in front of him. He laughed. The feeling was amazing. He fantasised about cutting hundreds of people down in a single action. He continued his fanciful cull, swishing the tool back and forth. He'd be a real god. A god that other gods bowed down to. He'd be awe-inspiring and not some pathetic loser.

Again, he ran the Scythe back and forth in the air. He'd be good at this, killing people. Maybe not as good as Jules, at least not at the beginning, but he'd soon perfect his technique and develop his own unique style. He could absolutely do this. He imagined rows of people in front of him and mowing them down. He imagined cutting Rachel down.

He suddenly felt sick. Jimmy let the Scythe drop to the ground, halting his imaginary harvest. Dizzy and nauseous he pressed his hand against his stomach, confused. Gods don't get food poisoning. They don't get flu or pick up parasites. Listlessly, he swung the Scythe through the air again. Rachel. She had to die. He had to kill her. Had to. And only the Scythe could do it.

He didn't actually want Rachel to leave. She was much better at Scrabble, which did annoy him, but he liked having her around. He enjoyed being responsible for her.

He couldn't kill her.

Rachel ran her hand along the row of DVDs; there were hundreds of them. All comedies: Laurel and Hardy, The Three Stooges, Bing Crosby and Bob Hope's *On the Road* collection. She closed her eyes and plucked one from the shelf.

"*Mr Bean's Holiday.*" She turned it over in her hand. "Do you actually like this stuff? I hate slapstick. It's so childish."

"It's actually quite sophisticated, I think you'll find. And requires a lot of skill to perform." Plucking the film from her hand, he put it back on the shelf.

"Really? Argh. All that faffing around. He stands up and knocks the other one down, who then in turn drops everything he's holding, which ruins all the work they've done. It's infuriating – can't they get anything right?"

"Precisely. Who can fall over at just the right moment to set a chain of chaos into action? Anyway, why should there be conditions on what makes you laugh? If it's funny, you laugh. I'll show you." Jimmy ran his finger along the shelf and pulled out *Duck Soup*. "Unless you're resisting, and that's a different thing."

"No, really, do we have to?" Rachel slumped down on the far end of the sofa and laid her head back, rolling it around like a small child avoiding the request to complete an unwelcome task.

"I promise you'll be laughing by the end. It's a classic."

"Usually that means tedious and out-dated. And why the DVDs? It's so old school."

"I like to collect physical objects." He placed the disc into the machine. "There's no harm in watching, is there? Give it a go, you might even enjoy it."

"Okay … I guess so. It might be nice not to have to think about anything."

"How gracious of you." He pressed play on the remote control and sat at the opposite end of the sofa as the music began.

Rachel was watching Jimmy laugh. It was always a loud outburst followed by silence, accompanied by him holding onto his stomach as if he had appendicitis, his entire body shaking as it bobbed up and down. Tears rolled down his cheeks and dripped onto his robe. This had been going on for the past forty-five minutes.

"How can anything be that funny?" Incredulous at the mess in front of her, Rachel stared. He made an attempt to control himself, breathing in hard, then panting noiselessly fast. Jimmy burst out laughing again and pointed at her, unable to form any words. He flapped his hands up and down as if it would steady him. Unable to help herself, her face cracked into a grin. Jimmy pointed at her again. She broke into laughter. Surprised, she attempted to compose herself.

"See! You're laughing," he accused her.

"At you, not the film," she corrected.

"It doesn't matter, you're still laughing. So it is the film. It made me laugh and that made you laugh."

"That's cheating." At the same moment they both burst into laugher again but a loud knock interrupted. Jimmy stopped immediately.

"We never get visitors …"

"Shush," Jimmy cut her off. He took long strides across the floor and stood behind the door.

"Who is it?" he shouted at the closed door.

"Cousin, your brother requires your attention. Immediately." The voice was female, unusually deep and soporific.

"Alright, I'll be along in a minute."

"He says I must return with you," the voice insisted.

"Does he? Well …"

"His mood is splenetic, James. May I enter?" Jimmy shoved his shoulder into the door as it started to open. It slammed shut.

"Obviously not," the voice continued.

"I'll come, just give me a second. I've been exercising." Rachel laughed and Jimmy glared at her.

"Do not jest. He is bellicose." The voice was stern.

"Okay, I'm coming." Jimmy stood up straight, smoothed his robe with both of his hands, turned to face the door, took a deep breath, and left the room.

Rachel had been shocked at the change in Jimmy. He'd gone from laughing to the point of asphyxiation to looking like the life was being drained from him. She was amazed he could get any paler. His brother must be a tyrant if he had that effect on him. When he'd told her about his brother, she'd underestimated how he felt. Now Rachel wasn't surprised that Jimmy was so nervous. And it didn't seem fair that his brother held him back so much. She'd only known him a few weeks but he was definitely more complex than she'd first thought. Families can be so difficult. Her mother had married within a year of her dad leaving, and although her stepdad was okay, it had been hard to adjust to life under a new regime. His authority was unwanted and she resented having her mother's attention taken away from her. Security was something she could no longer take for granted. Within a year her brother, Danny, had been born. The happy nuclear family complete with a gurgling junior made her feel like the cuckoo in her own nest. The result was she told them nothing and was determined to prove she could be a success without them. When, in her first year of university, she'd fallen pregnant she told no one and silently dealt with the problem alone. Surface infallibility was her protection. But it was such hard work to face everything alone. Rachel decided she'd find a way to help Jimmy. She would encourage him to confront his brother and get his job changed.

"You love her? Honest to goodness, Jimmy, this situation goes from bad to worse." Jules had become impatient at waiting for Jimmy's confession, but he'd never expected a declaration of love. He admitted to himself he couldn't understand Jimmy at all.

"I want her to stay here with us. For good."

Jimmy held his hands clasped together in front of him, anticipating disaster. He kept his gaze fixed on Jules's stationery; his pens were lined up on his desk in straight rows: everything he did was perfect. Death drew in a long breath. He'd been working on an official complaint from Odin that Minerva had interfered with his plans for war in the Middle East. She had counter claimed that he was "over zealous" and they could all do with a break. As if that wasn't enough, Dionysus was boring the Dryads with his tedious drunken stories. They complained he was no longer good company. Jesus had been hanging about his office too. He was a nice chap but Death wished he'd get to the point more directly: his stories were not the most efficient way of getting things done. Gods and their petty problems had been a constant burden to him. And now Jimmy. Again. Jules stared at him from the far side of his desk, affecting peaceful calm.

"Not only did you take the Scythe and attempted, poorly, I might add, to kill a human, but now this. How you thought I'd never notice is a mystery. I've allowed you enough rope and it's time to sort it out. And after all I said to you." Standing up, Death wasn't sure if he should shake Jimmy or not.

"I'm sorry. Sorry, sorry. Are you angry?" Jimmy kept his eyes lowered, looking at the ground.

"Not angry, just disappointed." Death contained his frustration, holding it back with the strength of his clenched jaw. Jimmy doubted he was "just disappointed".

"Does she love you?" Jules asked with a hint of derision.

"It's complicated."

"So what exactly is your plan? Hold her captive here until she starts asking uncomfortable questions?" Filling his pipe, the abundant tobacco spilled onto his tweed trousers. Jules brushed it from his trousers with the tips of his slender fingers. Similar to his immaculate house, he was impeccably attired. He only wore his robes when on duty and to keep up appearances. In looks, the brothers resembled one another, although Jules was confident, with the well-assembled air of a World War Two RAF hero.

"She never stops asking uncomfortable questions. I just thought she, well, she might learn to love me." Jimmy flopped into the chair opposite Jules.

"Learn to love you? You're holding her hostage." Jules struggled to contain his disbelief. "You've got to sort this out. She must be returned to the human world immediately, and don't tell her anything about your 'mistake' or where she is. If you haven't already. Just get rid of her. There will be consequences for this, and you've got to show me you're responsible. This is your last chance."

"No. I want Rachel. I knew you wouldn't understand – you've never been in love. You're prejudiced against her because she's human, and all that death has twisted your mind. You can't tell me what to do. I won't let you! She's staying with me."

"I will take her without argument if you don't return her to the human world *now*."

Death watched as his younger brother tripped on the hem of his robe, stumbled sideways, and regained his composure before storming off, slamming the door behind him. Death lit his pipe and inhaled. He had been patient, but he couldn't let Jimmy continue like this. Jimmy didn't understand the danger he was in. It was true, Death did have the power of life and death, but there was only so much he could do. It was his job to maintain the balance of things; his hands were tied. Jimmy never seemed to understand that. It was such a shame; Jimmy had such potential. And he was his own flesh and blood after all. But the laws were the laws; there was no negotiation over them. Being sent to earth to become a mortal, his life reduced to a flash in the pan – it just wasn't fitting for Death's brother. Death would become a laughingstock. He would give Jimmy one last chance to do the right thing and then he would have to act on his words.

Rachel was lying on her bed trying to think of ways to help Jimmy stand up to his brother. It was difficult without really knowing what he was like. She wondered if Jimmy would introduce her. There was a quiet knock on the door.

"Is that you, Jimmy?" She got up and opened the door.

"Can I come in?" His eyes pleaded.

"Of course. You've been ages. Is your brother hassling you again?" Jimmy shrugged and turned away from her.

"You've got to stand up to him. Demand he gives you what you want."

"You really don't know my brother, it's not that easy."

"Maybe I could meet him, get a better idea of what makes him tick?"

"No, no, Rachel, that's really not a good idea at all. Anyway, it's time to move on. Your fate has been decided."

"Oh." Rachel sat back on the bed and started flicking through the pages of a book.

"What does 'oh' mean? I thought you'd be pleased." He sat on the bed beside her.

"I am, but I'm starting to like it here." She kept her face turned away from him and continued plucking at the book.

"You do?" He grinned. "It's just, there are no other humans, only you. I thought you'd start to think it's strange that you're dead and there are no other dead people around." She lay back on the bed and put her arms behind her head.

"I don't mind, really." She rolled onto her side and propped up her head. It was true, she didn't mind. More than that, she was enjoying being freed from her innate talent of knocking the fun out of everything.

"Oh." He swallowed hard. "I'm so sorry. You have to move on, and I'm taking you."

"You're taking me? Okay, yes, at least that's something." She trailed off. He smiled and stood up to face her. "Where are we going?"

"To post-limbo. It's a training school for the afterlife. It will take us a couple of days to get there."

Instead of glorious sunshine, the moon shone bright and low, making the rose garden seem sinister and misshapen. It was odd that Jimmy had insisted they leave at night and bring very little with them but she didn't ask him any questions. He was so stressed about the journey it didn't seem fair to add to his worry. However, when he announced they'd be going on foot, she'd wondered how far they'd actually get. After having some time to think about it, "post-limbo" sounded a little odd too. But bringing it up at that moment would be awkward, Rachel decided.

Repeating his earlier ritual, Jimmy stuck his head out of the doorway before venturing onto the pathway. The glasshouses loomed over them, dominating the skyline. Rachel felt they were watching the two of them, ushering them along, keeping them to the pathway. Above them the ink black sky was pricked with silver pinholes. Rachel wanted to stop and indulge in the uniqueness of each constellation. Formations revealed only by the dark. But Jimmy was hustling her on, habitually looking behind him, as if he expected to be followed.

Rachel was tired. They'd been walking for a long time and Jimmy had barely said a word. Reaching a break in the glasshouses, they turned a corner and an allotment lay ahead. It was as regimented as the glasshouses, but instead there were hundreds of rows of vegetables. Vines hung from canes built into structures to support their growth. Every plant was heavy with pods or beans, bushy leaves sprouting from the ground. It was luscious.

At the far end of the garden was a row of brick sheds. Small white-framed windows spotted the walls at regular intervals. As they approached, Jimmy reached up and took a key down from the top of the doorframe. He opened the door, bobbing down to enter. Inside was a miniature living room. Everything was slightly too small for an average-sized man so Jimmy looked enormous. In the centre of the room was a round wooden table with two chairs on either side. Behind it was a Welsh dresser and, next to that, a deep china sink. A single tap hovered above it. Behind the door was a narrow bed dressed with rough blankets. Jimmy put his bag down and picked up the kettle. He filled it with water.

"Cup of tea?" He lit a small gas stove and placed the kettle on it.

"Yes please, I'm parched." Rachel flopped down at the table, her head collapsing onto her arms.

"Jimmy, what are we doing here?" He kept his back to her.

"Resting for the night."

She answered, unable to lift her head from fatigue. "Okay, but it all feels, well, a bit strange. It feels like we're running away."

Jimmy forced a laugh and turned around. "Of course not. Don't be silly."

"This place could be a secret hideout."

He sat down opposite her. The tops of his knees poked up over the table's surface.

"It's fine, Rachel. Enough." His voice was raised.

She'd never seen Jimmy angry before and she didn't like it.

Jimmy is walking along the street and everyone else is walking in the opposite direction. The pavement gets busier and people keep knocking into him. He starts to panic because he doesn't recognise anything or anyone, and the people look angry and mean and the jostling turns into pushing. A murmur permeates the crowds of people as they begin to whisper, "You can't run away, you can't escape". The whisper gets louder and louder until Jimmy shouts.

"Maude, get out of my head!"

Jimmy sat bolt up right and saw his cousin standing in front of his chair. "Why can't you just speak to me instead? The dream thing is too intimate."

Rachel stirred in the small camp bed. Jimmy held his breath, but Rachel turned over and continued to sleep.

"Apologies and do not worry cousin, I have given her a very pleasing dream. She will not wake. I needed to find you urgently and this is by far the speediest method." Her deep voice rumbled through the cottage.

"Are you sure about the dream? Let's go outside." Jimmy ushered Maude from the cottage and led her to the back of the garden.

"My quest is to, if possible, dissuade you from your foolhardy mission. You cannot outwit Death, and he is furious. You know this well, as do I. He will send you to live amongst the mortals. James, you will die as a mortal. Is this what you want?" Jimmy stared at the ground, refusing to look at her.

He didn't want to be mortal. A human's life was short and dull. Jimmy wanted to be a more impressive god with exciting powers. "I can see why Jules grows impatient with you. Do you want to give up your duties and forsake your family? There is no guarantee you will even know Rachel in the mortal world, and you will have given up everything for nothing in return. Where do you think you are even trying to go that Death will not follow?"

James kept his eye to the ground and mumbled, "To the love gods."

Maude frowned and lifted Jimmy's head up by his chin. "I cannot discern your words."

"TO THE LOVE GODS!" He folded his arms.

"Why you persist in acting like a human, I do not know. What help can they be to you?"

"Of course I don't want to be mortal, what's the point in that, as you say? But the love gods might know somewhere we can go to be together without HIM interfering."

"You are living in a world of dreams, James. You vex him at every turn." Jimmy smiled.

"A world of dreams. That's it, Maude! Maybe you could help us?"

"Do not even dare to think of it. You are my kin, James, and I love you, but even if I could sustain a dream that could be a home for you both, I would not dare to cross Death in such a way."

"You're here now, unless you're just his stooge, spying on us to tell him all about it."

"Oh James, I do not need to 'spy' as you say. I am attempting to help you keep your place amongst us, but I can see you need to learn your own lesson." Jimmy's shoulders slumped and his gown slipped around the top of his arm.

"Just keep him distracted until I can find out if there's a chance for us. I know he'll realise soon enough I haven't returned her yet, but help me. Please, Maude, please."

"I will try, but be swift in your task and promise me that if the love gods tell you that there is nothing that can legally be done, you will give up this pursuit." Jimmy grabbed Maude and hugged her tight.

Maude continued as she struggled free. "If you are in need of me, James, you know how I can be contacted. Sleep well."

*****

It had put Jimmy in a good mood that Maude had helped him. Being a bit of a swot and devoted to Jules, she could have gone either way. He'd never have such reservations about help from Hegemone or, as he'd told Rachel, "The Gardener". They'd been friends for years and both shared a love of growing things. Jimmy was pottering around the room when

Rachel opened her eyes. He took some plates down from the Welsh dresser and placed them with care on the table. In the centre was a basket piled with fresh bread rolls, and next to it a huge glass bowl overflowing with sumptuous summer fruits. Jimmy stood back and stared at the table arrangement as if admiring a work of art.

"Where did the food come from?"

Jimmy started as Rachel spoke. She laughed as Jimmy clutched at his chest. "You scared the life out of me. No need to laugh."

"Sorry, but your expression was a picture." Still laughing as she stood up, she reached over and plucked a fat cherry from the bowl. Struggling, he managed to rearrange his robe.

"Delicious cherries. And the bread smells amazing." Rachel grabbed a handful of fruit.

"The Gardener brought us the food. She's agreed to ..." He stopped. "Help" might suggest something was wrong.

"She? I thought The Gardener would be a man, with a big beard." Rachel indicated a beard by rubbing her chin.

"Sexist." Jimmy pretended to pull on it.

"She's agreed to what?"

"Nothing, just gave us some provisions. For the journey."

"We did leave in a bit of a hurry, under the

cloak of night."

"I just wanted to get a head … a good start."

"On foot?" Rachel pointed to her thin leather ballet pumps. Jimmy grinned at her.

"Look outside."

Rachel moved to the door and pulled it open. Parked across the entrance of the cottage was a wooden cart. A chestnut brown horse stood tethered at its front. The horse lifted its head and looked at her for a brief moment and then returned to munching on a bucket of oats.

"Mademoiselle, your carriage awaits." As he spoke, Jimmy gave Rachel a deep bow.

Rachel clung to the seat of the cart as a jolt sent her left and a lurch flung her to the right. Each rock or pothole threatened to shake the cart into pieces.

"This is glorious, don't you think, Rachel." It was a statement, not a question. Any trace of stress and urgency Jimmy had shown the previous night was gone.

"Yeah, if you like being shaken to the bone." Rachel momentarily lost her grip of the seat as the cart rolled into a hole. First the front and then the back wheel dropped and lurched before it levelled itself. Rachel scrambled, trying to regain her grasp and tentative security.

"The open road." Jimmy gestured ahead.

"Dirt track," Rachel corrected. Jimmy ignored Rachel's comment and continued.

"Sunshine." He raised his hand to the sky, indicating the sun. Rachel couldn't deny the sun was shining, and it was very warm. She couldn't even claim a cloud.

"We've delicious provisions."

Okay, yes, the food *was* delicious.

"And the best company."

He smiled at Rachel. Jimmy had that annoying way of always seeing the bright-side, and, most annoying of all, making her see the best in things. It was infectious and she was happy to be infected. She smiled back at him. On one side of the road was thick green forest and on the other fields of gold and lavender. It was beautiful and smelled delicious. She had to concede, despite the quality of the cart ride, they were having an adventure.

The sun had almost disappeared, leaving a smudge of orange lingering above the tree-tops, when Jimmy turned the cart into a clearing. A huge stone temple stood in front of them. It was dark and looming.

"This is where we'll be staying for the night. I've got a few friends that live here. They'll put us up."

"In the Acropolis?" Rachel laughed.

Jimmy pulled the horse's reigns to the left, directing the cart around the side. It seemed to

Rachel the temple was miles long, but soon she could hear the sound of music and the chatter of multiple voices. Permeating the air was the smell of roasting meat. As they turned the corner, yet another immaculate garden lay in front of them. Fruit trees were scattered amongst a sea of colourful flowers and thick foliage bordered a wide path. Two figures strolled side by side, their heads close together in intense conversation. To the left, connected to the building with a covered portico, was a terrace that resembled an open-air drawing room. A small group of people were standing or lying on stone benches arranged around a fire. Figures were draped in white cloth, which hung from their bodies in elaborate folds. Intricate embroidery in red, blue and gold adorned the edges. A young man with a headful of dark curls was playing a soft tune on a lyre. Stars appeared, bright in the darkening sky, as the last of the sun faded. Rachel stood a step behind Jimmy as he stopped at the periphery of the gathering.

"Pothos, it isn't all about yearning and sexual desire. Love is kind, patient and loyal."

A slender youth rose from his seat and approached the older woman who'd been speaking. He touched his hand to his breast as he spoke.

"But the pleasure of yearning for your love object is so intense, so bittersweet. It's delicious."

"You forget, I know the cruelty and pain of being parted from the one I love."

"How could we forget, Demeter? It defines you."

"The love of a mother is uncond—"

"Unconditional. Yes, yes. You've told us. I think the only love that truly matters is for oneself," interrupted another beautiful youth who was looking at himself in a hand mirror.

"How tiresome you are, Narcissus. But what have we here?" Pothos moved across the square towards Jimmy. He recognised him immediately and stepped forward, his arms outstretched.

"Jimmy. It's been such a long time, I've missed you." Pothos clasped Jimmy in his arms and held him tight. "And who is this beautiful creature?"

"Welcome, my dear." Demeter removed Rachel's hand from Pothos's grip. "You must be a friend of Jimmy's."

"We've only known each other a few weeks, but I guess so." Jimmy blushed. Demeter and Pothos exchanged glances.

"You see what I mean, Demeter? The sweet joy of longing."

"It's not like that at all." Rachel laughed, giving Jimmy a gentle push. Again, Jimmy blushed.

"Anyway, I'm dead, and we're on the way to the afterlife." All of the gods' eyes shifted to Jimmy.

"How can that be, Jimmy?" Demeter frowned.

"I'm doing Death a favour. He made a mistake and I'm just trying to fix it." Jimmy avoided Demeter's eye.

"Since when does Death make mistakes?"

Jimmy forced a laugh. "We're all human." He attempted another laugh at his own joke and turned away to pick up two goblets. "Wine, Rachel? You must be thirsty?"

Again, the gods looked at one another.

"You must be tired after your journey. We're being rude. Will you join us for some refreshments? Sit, eat, drink." An array of dishes were paraded in front of her: roasted meats, olives, bread and fresh fruit. Rachel helped herself. Two figures who had been sitting quietly in the corner following the conversation now stood up. One of them addressed her.

"Don't you think love should be harmonious, Rachel?" He pulled his mane of hair away from his face.

"It never is. Even the people who should love you have their own agenda."

Anteros smiled and tilted his head, his hair falling, abundant, over one shoulder. "And if you could take your revenge on the people who didn't love you in the way you need, would you?"

Rachel stopped chewing and thought for a moment. "I'd like them to know how it feels to be pushed out and isolated." She looked to Jimmy, thinking of how his brother treated him, how her family treated her.

"What do you think, Jimmy?" Anteros switched his gaze to Jimmy.

"I don't know."

"Really?" Anteros urged.

Jimmy shuffled his feet. "I guess I think you can't punish someone for how they feel – or don't feel. But that's not the point, you're having the wrong argument – all types of love are embedded with fear, longing and grief – or it's not love. You're all saying that in your own way. I think loving someone is yours, it's how you feel, and whether it's returned or not isn't the point; it's not under control. Pain is part of that." Everyone was silent until Demeter moved forward and put her arms around Jimmy.

"Unconditional love," she murmured contentedly.

"If love is not equally matched on both sides, what's the point?" Anteros was insistent. Jimmy snorted. It was typical of the love gods to misunderstand. Shallow and blinkered, they could only see love from their own individual perspectives, but then that was their job, even if it was infuriating.

The second figure, who had yet to speak, stood up and took Jimmy's arm, walking him a few paces towards the entrance to the temple.

"What do you think, Albina?" asked Jimmy.

"Ill-fated lovers are the saddest of all. However much love is between them, circumstances are against them. Good night Jimmy, I shall return with the dawn."

Hidden behind a pillar, Jimmy watched as a golden slither trailed across the deep-blue hues of the night garden. Albina moved with grace, delicate swirls glowed behind her. She stopped, collected the light in both hands, and launched it into the air. A chink of orange appeared on the horizon to the east.

"It's okay, Jimmy, you can come out. I know you're there." He crept from behind the pillar and cautiously stepped into the emerging dawn. He tripped on the lyre that had been left the previous evening. Its strings called out as if in pain as it toppled over onto the ground. As he got close to her, she held out her hands and led him deeper into the garden and away from the temple.

"I know why you're here, Jimmy."

"You do?" Jimmy gulped.

"It's obvious you're in love with her, and you want my protection. You seek to stay together."

Jimmy nodded. "I didn't plan on falling in love with her but there you have it. Now I have and I need your help."

"The only way, legally speaking, is if she goes back to the mortal world and you continue on your path of defying Death and become mortal. As a human, you wouldn't be you, as you are now, and there's no guarantee you'd know each other, let alone be in love."

"No, I don't want that. I want Rachel to stay here. Isn't there some way to keep her here?"

"Not that I know of. I'm sorry, Jimmy."

Jimmy sat on a bench, folding his arms around his body. Albina sat down next to him. Together they watched as sunlight broke through the trees.

"He knows everything you've done, Jimmy. He's waiting for you to do the right thing. You know that, don't you?"

"I hate him. This is all his fault. He wouldn't let her stay and he doesn't understand that I'm capable of more. He wants me to do the 'right thing', as you say, so he doesn't have the shame of having to send me down. That's all. This is all about him. As usual."

"He loves you, Jimmy, and he has such a lot on his shoulders."

Jimmy stood up and shouted, "You're supposed to be the Protector of Ill-Fated Lovers. You're supposed to help! But what good are you? You're as bad as he is." Tears rolled down Jimmy's face and dripped onto his robe.

"You're right, I'm sorry. Death is too powerful and Rachel is here illegally. He will separate you in the end. I can offer some sanctuary, but not long term. I can get you some time to talk to the other love gods and find out if they have any solutions."

Rachel thought about what she'd heard as she crawled back through the bushes. The conversation about death didn't make any sense to her, and Jimmy was upset with his brother again. He'd also said he loved her. Rachel was surprised; it hadn't occurred to her. They were becoming good friends and she liked him, but love was not what she'd expected, not at all. When alive she wouldn't have liked him; he was far too awkward. But being in limbo had given her the chance to be herself, the person she was beneath all the nonsense and work of being alive, and Jimmy had been a large part of that. She was grateful to and fond of Jimmy; it was an unusual relationship she'd never experienced before. But she was sure it wasn't love. When alive she didn't have these problems because she didn't have these feelings.

Rachel didn't stand up until she reached the temple and was sure neither Jimmy nor Albina had seen her.

Pretending to be asleep, Rachel kept her arm over her face so Jimmy couldn't see her eyes as he re-entered the room. Pouring himself a goblet of wine, he dropped it, spilling it on his robe. The goblet clanked numerous times as it bounced on the stone floor. Rachel took advantage of his mistake and pretended to stir from her sleep, stretching her arms and sitting up. She rubbed her eyes to complete the façade.

"Sorry, sorry, sorry. Go back to sleep." Fumbling with a cloth to mop up the liquid, Jimmy was down on all fours.

"What on earth are you doing up at the crack of dawn?"

"I just needed a drink."

She was disappointed at his logical answer. He'd need drawing out. "You look upset. Is everything okay?"

He continued mopping. "Yes, why wouldn't it be? I'm just fed up with spilling things and falling over things and making a mess of everything." This was great. He was one step away from confession. Jimmy smiled.

"Well, not everything." He paused. "How would you feel about staying here a bit longer?"

"Everyone seems nice. Mostly. If a little love-obsessed. But why? I thought we were on our way to the other side."

"A change of plans."

"Another? You never tell me what's really going on. Besides, this is *my* death, and I don't think it's going so well. I had no idea it would be so complicated."

"I thought we were having a good time – an adventure." He slumped into a sitting position on the floor. He looked pitiful.

"Yes, I suppose, but I'm beginning to think it's all a bit fishy."

"Fishy?"

"I think you keep things from me, and that's not friendship in my book." Rachel thought that was a bit harsh and Jimmy looked sad, like a crumpled teacloth waiting to go into the washing machine, but she couldn't relent. He was quiet for a few minutes.

"Rachel, you know how I told you that you got killed by mistake?"

"Yes." She was puzzled.

"And that I was waiting to hear for orders as to what to do?"

"Yes."

"Well …" He flinched, afraid of his confession.

"Jimmy, just spit it out."

"I killed you, and it was up to me to sort it out. I'm really, really sorry." Jimmy hid his face behind his enlarged hand.

"You killed me? How?" Now she was perplexed.

"I borrowed the Scythe from my brother, and instead of a panic attack, you … died." He closed his eyes, waiting to be told off.

"Death's your brother!?"

"You've got two choices."

"Choices? I thought death was kind of final."

"Normally, yes, but officially Death didn't take you. I did, and it's not my job. Jules says I have to sort it out. So here we are."

"Death is called Jules?"

Two choices. If she decided to return to her life she would remember nothing of what had happened to her in limbo, and all her anxieties that had drifted away over the previous weeks would return.

Or, she could choose what was behind door number two and go with Death to the other side. But there was no knowing what was over there. Jimmy didn't know: not his department.

She was furious with him. Her death hadn't been a doctor's mistake but his mistake. And Death was his brother – no wonder he wasn't very flexible. But he'd also said to Albina that he loved her and was trying to find a way to keep them together. And he still hadn't revealed his true feelings about her.

Watching him, a pathetic lump slumped on the floor, made her anger subside. Feeling sorry for him meant she couldn't stay angry with him, even if he had lied about almost everything.

"You got me into this, Jimmy, and I think it's only fair you help me out of it." Rachel sat next to him, and gently stroked his shoulder. "Tell me everything about this place, who you are and what you do. I'm guessing you're not The Caretaker. Is there even such a thing?"

Jimmy shook his head. "I'm sorry, Rachel. I just wanted to do something more important and show Jules he could trust me and then …" He trailed off.

"And then what?"

"It just got out of hand." He turned to her and for the first time looked her dead in the eyes. "Rachel, I need to show you what I really do."

The hall contained row upon row of small bell-shaped glass jars. Each jar had a square white label stuck on the front, displaying a name and date. It was dark; sporadic rays of light fell across the shelves where the curtains had holes and tears. Dust rotated in the air, catching the light and sparkling like glitter. Jimmy switched on the lights; they blinked on one after the other across the huge expansive ceiling.

"It's everyone's bad emotions, their anxiety and negativity." Rachel followed him further into the room. She strained her neck trying to see how high the shelves were stacked."

"But there are so many of them."

"There are a lot of people. Everyone suffers from time to time to a greater or lesser extent, but mostly people live a benign existence. There has to be an adequate happy/sad balance in the universe and when you get a spike either way it skews that balance. Sadness and happiness are linked and a person's ability to lead a rewarding life means being able to experience a range of emotions. If a jar fills beyond a certain level and quantity, I step in."

"Step in?"

"Yeah, well, panic attacks, red mists, you know all too well what I mean. I manage the misery process. Some people can't deal with pain and pretend they're okay, so panic attacks are there to raise the stakes, push people into getting help. I've been seeing to you for a while now." He looked pleased.

"Thanks very much, but really there was no need."

"Oh, no problem." He realised he was actually enjoying explaining to her how his job worked. "While you're suffering, you feel like you're the only one, but clearly you're not. That's just ridiculous."

"Are you saying I'm ridiculous?" Rachel was hurt.

"No, never. It's just the way the process works. To avoid a contagion, the suffering is very much restricted to the individual. You can't see what's going on in someone else's mind." He quietly laughed.

"A personal service delivered just about anywhere."

"Yeah." Jimmy laughed louder. "People think they're alone in their misery. They think people won't understand, or that they're a bother, or worst of all, boring others with their problems. Look at the way your parents are with you. So sufferers never share their feelings, which then heightens them. It's up to each individual to seek help. You know, you have to want to get better. It's a cycle. Good, isn't it?" He was beaming at her.

"I don't think 'good' is quite the right word," Rachel scolded.

"No, you're quite right, sorry. It's not good. It's clever."

"Clever but cruel." She turned away from him and walked along the rows of shelves, trailing her hand across the dusty jars. It was clever, and the balance had been maintained because of him. He'd done a good job as long as humans had suffered, and that was as long as they'd existed. The nature and cause of suffering may have changed through time, but it invariably ended up the same way: with insecurity and anxiety, fear and depression, panic, confusion and loneliness. Suffering had a long list of symptoms and Jimmy was the master of maintaining them all.

"But what about me, then? Where are my jars?"

He led her to the back of the storage facility. There were four doors. He approached the one on the far right.

"These cases are currently active." Pulling out

an enormous bunch of keys from the pocket of his robe, he fumbled with the key ring until he found the correct one and unlocked the door. This room was smaller and cleaner, the jars were brightly coloured and completely full. He led her around a corner into an alcove. There were four shelves filled with jars that were labelled with her name.

"There are loads of them, I had no idea … but look at them, what does it mean?" She took a jar down from the shelf and read the label: *Rachel Stone: 1994, Parents break up*. She read the next one: *Father moves to Australia*; the next one: *Mother remarries*; the next one: *Birth of half-brother*; and the final one: *2000, Abortion*.

Rachel was stunned.

"What does this … please, I don't understand." She was sobbing.

"Your panic attacks, your sense of hopelessness, what do you think caused them?"

"I'm not well, I'm ill, I'm going to … I'm dead …"

"By accident."

"Yes, but, crowded places, they're hot, all those people, anything could happen."

"Not everyone feels like that in seedy night spots, unbelievable as it sounds."

"You're lying! I love my family, and the abortion was the right thing to do." Tears were running down her face. She wiped her nose on her sleeve.

"That may be true, but it's not that simple. Human emotion is complex."

"How the hell do you know? You're not even human."

"But I know you, Rachel. You pretend to be tough but you've been through all these horrible things and never allowed yourself to be sad or even given yourself a break."

Rachel slipped to the ground in a crumpled mass. What he said was true. Her fear had become a mask for her grief. Fear of accidents and disaster were a deflection from her disappointments and sadness. Jimmy sat beside her. Snot ran from her nose like two veins of lava. She whimpered.

"I thought being successful and in control would protect me from pain, but I can't get away from it anywhere. I'm better off dead."

"I wouldn't want you to die."

"You killed me."

"That was then. You could have a great life, Rachel, if only you could see that everything is okay. You're enough."

"But everything is always so hard all of the time. I've struggled for everything I've got, everything I've achieved, clamouring, determined to be slimmer, cleverer, more exciting, more accomplished, just better than I actually am. Desperate to show everyone how perfect I can be." Once again

Rachel sobbed.

"I don't want to sound smug …"

"Then don't," she snapped through a sniff.

"But you've been happy here, I think."

"I'm dead, that doesn't count."

"You've been happy because you haven't had to try. We've played games, travelled, enjoyed –" He wanted to say being together but continued with "– nature and good food. We've just been living. And it's been good, great even."

Her sobs subsided and she stared at him. "So I'm better off here, dead."

"Except you're not actually dead. You still have a chance to live."

"Why can't I stay here?"

"It's against the rules. You're not a god or associated being."

"Okay then. If I really have to choose, I want to know what Death is like. I want to see him."

"Why on earth? You know what he'd do. To both of us."

"I've got nothing to lose, have I? It might make it easier to, you know, make a decision."

"You can't look Death in the eye and come away the same person, he's very imposing if you're not used to it, I don't …"

"Jimmy, please." She touched his hand. Jimmy gave a small shiver as the touch went through him.

"There's one thing we could do."

"What?"

"He has a nap at three every afternoon."

"A nap?"

"We'd have to be really quiet, and quick. In and out, like lightning."

Death's bedroom was cosy, wood-panelled and dominated by a huge, canopied four-poster bed. Rachel guessed Tudor. The curtains and furnishings were matching, expensive, red velvet. A large stuffed raven, wings outstretched, kept guard above the bed. Rachel and Jimmy hovered behind the heavy oak door, attempting to see through the gap between the door and its frame.

"He's really into home design, every room is from a different period of history. He says decorating helps him to relax and takes his mind off things."

"I wish it helped me."

"It's never the same when you do something for a living." He shrugged his shoulders at her. "He's asleep." Death was snoring so loudly that each time he exhaled, the glass on his bedside shook. His mouth hung open.

"I can see the family resemblance. He's sort of handsome, despite the loose jaw."

Jimmy frowned. "Really? Thanks, I think."

He tentatively pushed the door open. It squeaked.

He froze. Death stirred, and turned over. "Quick, go and look at him, then let's get out of here."

Rachel stepped out from behind Jimmy, slowly placing her foot gently on the thick carpet. She approached the bed and stopped a few feet away from his head.

"Not too close." Jimmy hissed a warning. Rachel kept going and shook Death by the arm.

"No! Rachel, stop!" He ran forward and pulled her away. In her confusion, her foot caught and tangled on the bottom of his robe. She lurched forward, Jimmy automatically holding out his hand to catch her. But her momentum was too strong and she fell forward onto her face, squealing in pain as Jimmy landed on top of her. Jimmy accidentally lent on her arm.

"Ouch, Jimmy, be bloody careful."

Death, slowly rising up from the bed, expanded his form as if a bird of prey spreading its wings. He filled the room. Booming, he shouted, staring down at the confused mass on the floor.

"What is going on here?" The glass in the window frame shook. He glowered at Jimmy struggling on the floor, tangled in arms and legs and clothes and hair. And Rachel crushed beneath him.

Jimmy stood up; Rachel followed, taking refuge behind him. Death was irate and their performance wasn't helping.

"Do you think you are The Two Stooges?"

"I think you'll find there were three–" Jimmy regretted his interruption immediately.

"Be quiet! James, you've defied me one too many times." Death maintained his engorged body.

Rachel stepped forward, keeping her eyes lowered. "It wasn't Jimmy's fault, it was mine. I made him bring me here. He didn't know my intention to wake you. I'm really sorry, but please don't blame Jimmy. He was just trying to make things easier on me."

Death was confused; he looked at Rachel and then at Jimmy.

"Is this true, James?"

"No, it was my idea. I thought it would help her choose." He stepped in front of Rachel, pushing his chest out.

"Don't do this, Jimmy. It was my fault. Please believe me." Rachel pulled at his shoulder to get in front.

"You two are as bad as each other. If, as you say Rachel, this is your fault then I've no choice."

"No, please, Jules. I don't want her to die."

Death shook his head at Jimmy. He turned to Rachel, ready to complete his promise.

In a panic, she shouted, "I don't want to die either. I want to go back. Jimmy may have made some terrible decisions but he's helped me to understand my problems and shown me that life doesn't always have to be a miserable struggle. I get it now." Her voiced calmed. "Life's not perfect. It's beautiful but it's not perfect. And that mess and ugliness, that pain and confusion, heightens all that is good. When life's a mess, the best way to solve it is not through perfection. Or using death to avoid it." She turned to Jimmy.

"Jimmy, you're an incredible person and I hope you can believe that about yourself too. You are perfect the way you are. And you have beautiful hands." Rachel slipped her hands into Jimmy's and kissed his enlarged knuckles. "Even this one."

As usual, Jimmy blushed, but beneath the red his relief made him feel as if he could stand up straight after years of carrying his worries on his back. Rachel continued. "I love you, Jimmy. You've made me happy. But I must face my fears and hopefully that means we won't see each other again. If I'm well, that is." Jimmy clasped her by the shoulders. The weight once again pressed on him.

"Don't go, please. I'll come with you, I'll become a mortal and find you."

"Amongst 7 billion people." Death reminded him dryly, now back to his normal size.

"No Jimmy, we both need to live. You're good at what you do and the universe needs you. I'm going to live the best life I can and maybe I'll see you in a few decades. Maybe then we can have something together."

He wanted to cry and stamp his feet but instead he clasped Rachel, holding her in a tight embrace. Anger gave way to contentment and slowly conceded to sadness. It paralysed him. At last, he'd got what he wanted and she loved him, but she had chosen life. That was what he wanted for her, but not without him. He wasn't sure if he could ever forgive her.

Death wiped away the tear that rolled down his face to the bottom of his chin.

*****

Rachel sank backwards into the leather sofa, and it consumed her, sucking her in. A drunken couple fell across her, kissing with wide mouths and visible tongues. Her ears flinched at each beat of the music; it merged with the sounds of human exhilaration into silence. The couple became an indistinguishable outline, blending and fading into blackness. Rachel's body lost power. She tried to stand but fell to the floor. Crawling forward, she grasped onto a pair of legs. Jimmy lifted his hand, taking it away from the top of her head. After a moment's pause, he leaned forward and lovingly kissed her on the cheek. That was the last time he'd visit her. It would be too painful otherwise. That's what his love demanded from him. Besides, he was sure she'd now have the strength to get help.

He looked around the bar and walked through the room to sit next to a toned and tanned man in his early twenties. His group of friends were all laughing and swigging from pint glasses. Jimmy placed his hand on the man's head and whispered:

"It won't be obvious now, but at some point you'll understand that I'm helping you."

"It sounds as if you've been experiencing a high level of anxiety for a prolonged period." The psychologist leaned forward, offering Rachel a tissue. "What do you think made you realise you need help?"

Rachel licked the flow of tears from her top lip. She attempted to speak, but the sound constricted in her throat.

"Take your time."

"I … I don't know. It doesn't seem normal for someone of my age to worry so much about everything."

Writer Biography

Sarah Gray has been storytelling all her professional life. As a writer and filmmaker she loves to explore the dark and comic sides of life.

Half Life is her second collection of short stories and she is currently working on her third. She lives in London.

9 781910 461174